D1537246

MARRIED TO THE ROCKSTAR

A Mile High Rocked Novel

CHRISTINA HOVLAND

For rights information, please contact:
Prospect Agency
551 Valley Road, PMB 377
Upper Montclair, NJ 07043
(718) 788-3217

Holly Ingraham, Development Editor
Audrey Nelson, Copy Editor
Shasta Schafer, Final Proofreader

Cover Model Photography by:
Eric McKinney / 6:12 Photography
Jason D., Cover Model

First Edition April 2022

For everyone who has ever thought they didn't deserve a happily ever after.

Yes, you do.

Chapter One
IRINA

IRINA CARMICHAEL LOVED little more than planning a good party. That one thing she adored more? Her nearly nonexistent, dehydrated excuse of an acting career. A soon-to-be rehydrated acting career, if the plan went well. A career she would nurture, cherish, and water like nobody's business.

For now, she focused on her upcoming publicity stunt of a wedding. Super-fake in the love sense, but very real in the legal sense, and hopefully enough to give her career the jump-start it needed.

They were two days away from the big engagement news drop—a carefully positioned leak to the tabloids to spill the news. They'd thought about a big proposal. She'd even pitched it to the groom, because who wouldn't want that? But in the end everyone worried it'd be too in-your-face and obvious.

"This is a lot of effort for an event that doesn't really count," Jeremy "Knox" Dillion—her friend and groom-to-be —said. He sat on the floor of the Denver, Colorado house they currently shared with her best friend Courtney and Courtney's guy, Knox's bandmate, and their baby. Currently they were babysitting little Harley so her mom and dad could catch a breather.

Baby Harley wasn't even a year old yet as she hung out in her green giraffe bouncy seat. Knox strummed his guitar for her as Irina worked at the table with two planners, three kinds of scissors, stickers out the nose, and a stack of bridal magazines. Not to mention a Venti Vanilla Frappuccino.

"You're barely paying attention." It's true, he was extremely uninvolved with the wedding planning, giving only cursory head nods and the occasional mm-hmm. Even when she'd been the one entertaining Ms. Harley with decisions about napkin color and lighting options.

"True." He didn't look up. "But I still notice, and I gotta say, you only need to put in about half the effort and you'll still get the results."

"Look," Irina said. "I'm probably only going to have three or four weddings in my entire life." She stapled a piece of cloth she intended for bridal gowns to her vision board. Well, it'd started to cover the entire wall, so it was more of a vision mural. But who was keeping track? "I want to make each one count."

She used to harbor fantasies about happily-ever-after with the man of her dreams, but she'd fallen in love early and they'd ended up breaking each other's hearts. Best not to get feelings involved, she discovered.

Knox harrumphed as a response and went back to strumming on his guitar. Saying something under his breath, and then grumbling about the strings before going back to his notes.

"If you didn't have the tour coming up, then we wouldn't be on such a tight schedule, hmm," Irina sang the words, working them in with the few bars he'd been fighting with for the past hour.

Knox was tall—really tall—with blond hair he kept a touch too long, and a muscled body that made a girl want to touch it all over. He lived his life as a rock star. Specifically, keyboardist for the insanely popular Dimefront. Though he was officially on the keyboards, he also played guitar. And today he'd spent the entire afternoon drafting what he assured her was a new hit single. She believed him because she'd been listening—the song was excellent.

He even had Harley cooing.

Irina loved spending time with Harley and her mama. Her dad Bax wasn't too bad, either. But Irina missed her life in Los Angeles. Not that she had tons of work there, which was why she needed an exposure boost to launch her career. Knox needed an image makeover since the paparazzi had branded him a big ol' jerk of a player. This marriage of convenience between them was created with the hope it could fix both of their issues.

"Hey, are you going to write me a song for the wedding?" she asked, because a wedding song would be super kick-ass and a very nice addition to the soirée. She eyeballed a different shade of emerald green for the flower girl dresses— tone on tone might be perfection—as she spoke.

"Wasn't planning on it," he mumbled with a pen clenched between his teeth. "You want one?"

"Uh-huh. Bax wrote Courtney a song. Lynx wrote Becca one, too." These pairings were also genuine couples who had fallen in love. The home they stayed in was Bax and Courtney's, across the street from Lynx and Becca. Up the way, at the end of the cul-de-sac, was Knox's current renovation project. He'd bought the house from a couple who had a lot of cats that peed on the pink carpet regularly. The whole place did not smell good, and it was *super* pink. Not cute pink, either.

Once they got married and the renovations were through, Irina would stay there sometimes for the photo ops, but the true love thing? No. That's not what Knox and Irina had. They were friends who got along well enough to get married, and he was wicked hot. Her goals did not align with a love match and neither did his, so it all worked out.

Who had time for love when there were future block-busters to get callbacks on?

"Courtney had Bax's baby." Knox strummed a few chords, nodded, then wrote something on the lined music pad. "Becca puts out on the regular," he continued. "That's why they got songs. You wanna have my baby or put out for me?"

Hold up. She and Knox didn't need to get carried away with things. She was neither going to put out or have his baby. But…

"I'll put *up* with you since I'm marrying you!" This was a big deal. Banks would link his credit to hers, she'd be legally responsible as his next of kin, and if he went to prison, she'd be the one who had to visit!

Again, an enormous deal.

"We are *both* getting what we want out of this." He glanced up, grinning that wicked smile of his. That smile and those dimples were the kind of thing that got him in trouble. The abs and the talent didn't hurt the total package situation either.

Knox took some serious heat in the tabloids for being the only original Dimefront band member still single and playing the field. It didn't help that every time he turned around the tabloids were twisting something he said or did to make him look like he really was a player and a jerkface.

Sure, Dimefront had added two new guys to the stage. But they were still wet behind the ears—no one expected them to settle down and fall in love. Not when the groupies tossed themselves in their direction like confetti from a cannon.

But Knox? He was being branded as a player since he'd had his confetti days, and the world now wanted to see *his* love match.

The branding him as a player thing? Totally hysterical,

because he actually was not a player. Knox was a good guy with a heart so big sometimes she wondered how he wasn't head over heels in love for real.

Anyhoo, this was the point at which Irina strode onto the stage.

An actress in need of some Hollywood-style attention meets a rock star in need of a partner.

Enter Courtney, Irina's best friend *and* a publicity professional, who suggested a marriage of convenience.

They'd both agreed, and ta-da they were doing this thing.

"What if I bake you something?" she suggested. Her kitchen skills actually held up. While most actresses took wait-staff positions, she worked in the kitchen. She could bake for him while he wrote her some lyrics. Ba-da-bing. Ba-da-boom.

"Now we are talking." Knox rubbed his hands together, his eyes positively sparkling.

She liked the sparkle thing, and it didn't hurt that Knox was a looker. With his a-little-too-long rocker hair and his California boy tan skin, he'd be perfect for the wedding photos. *Oh yeah.* Not to mention the blue eyes that made women throw their bras at him on the regular. She'd even considered it on more than one occasion during a weak moment or two.

"Any requests from the kitchen?" she asked, circling back to the baking for a song option.

He scrawled something on the paper and followed it with a tapa-tap-tap against the guitar. "How long does the song need to be?"

"At last two verses and a refrain." Not that she'd given it a ton of thought…only a little thought.

He pushed his hands in his hair, slicking it back. "You're killing me here."

She pressed her hands against her hips. "My job as your future wife is to harass you."

He gave her a not-buying-it look. Which, whatever, he

could think what he wanted. It's what she convinced him to do that mattered. Luckily, she was a professional at convincing.

"Any specialties in the kitchen?" he asked.

Uh. Yes. "I'm good with scones."

He lifted the side of his lip into a semi-cute baby snarl. "What are we? At high tea with the Queen? Do I look like a guy who eats scones?"

In all the time she'd known him, she'd actually never seen him eat a scone. Clearly, scones were a no go. But he did like—

"Pie?" she asked. She'd seen him on more than one occasion with an entire pie and a fork.

"Pie." He nodded.

"What kind?" He hadn't shown a particular preference, as far as she could tell.

"I enjoy all pie. Strawberry. Blueberry. Chocolate. Chocolate French silk. Banana cream. Key lime." He made a *slurp* sound. "Put it in a flaky crust and I'll devour it."

She'd sent her libido to sleep ages ago so she could focus on her career, but, uh, the way his gaze landed on her when he said the word "devour"? Her nerve endings all woke right the hell up, immediately putting her on the sexual defensive. So much so that she nearly said something about flaky crust mirroring his choice in women. But since she was the lady du jour, and he wasn't actually a player, it didn't really track.

"Just be sure the crust isn't soggy." He made a yuck face, because he obviously hadn't felt that uncomfortably sexual shift in the room. "That'll ruin everything. Even more than runny filling."

"Well, Pie Boy," she said, brushing aside an uncomfortable ache low in her belly. "I will happily make you pie for a song."

"Just a pie?" He tickled Harley's tummy, set his guitar aside. Stood. Moved to the piano. "Uh-uh. Lots of pie."

"Define lots?" As a unit of measure they could interpret it many, many ways.

He tapped a little ditty on the ivories, nodded, then did it again. "At least six. Different flavors."

Oh, is that how he was going to play this? "Three verses, one refrain, and a drum solo."

That got his attention.

"Serious? You're going to make me write a drum solo?"

"Yup." She sauntered toward him to prove to herself the sexual energy pulse was nothing more than a blip. "I love the drums."

Knox had balked ever so briefly at the engagement idea. During those moments, she'd started negotiations with Tanner—the Dimefront drummer. Tanner could hardly speak to a female without seizing up, but he'd been on board. Funny that… Irina hadn't been as excited to have him as her pretend husband. Tanner was sweet, but he wasn't Knox. In the end, though, his agreement spurred Knox into saying yes. Sometimes Irina just liked to mess with Knox a little and remind him that Tanner was happy to do the matrimony-for-press gig with her.

"Fine," he said as a grunt.

"And while we are on pie," she whispered, giving a glance to Harley, but the munchkin was nearly off to dreamland.

Irina traced her fingertip along the top of the piano. Blurgh, she hated having to say this, but they were going for good publicity, not terrible publicity. So she needed to lay it all out. "We need to discuss your need to refrain from lady pie, unless your, uh, friend signs a nondisclosure agreement," she said, quietly.

He stopped playing the piano and looked her straight in the eye. She hated when he did that because it always made her feel so…seen.

Not just as an actress or someone who loves the spotlight —but really seen. The dirt and grit, along with the gloss. The last guy who'd done that? Well… it'd ended badly for them both.

"NDA? That's gonna put a crimp in my pickup game," Knox said, low and mellow. Again that prickle of desire tugged at her.

She ignored it once more, and softly snort-laughed. "Like you have a game."

"I have loads of game." He feigned shock, but they both knew it wasn't true.

She leaned in to rebalance the scales, because it hadn't gone past her notice that he was a breast guy, and she was struggling way more than he was with the whole turned on thing. Leaning in this way would give a little cleavage boost to her standing in this conversation. "Then why are you marrying *me*?"

Ha. He totally checked out her girls before saying, "Because I don't hate you."

"Thanks." She rolled her eyes.

"Besides, are you getting an NDA before any games of hide the salami?"

Uh-huh. "One, don't call it that. Two, yes. Three, it doesn't matter because I'm actually planning on being celibate during our time together." Her insides all seemed to whine at that announcement.

He scowled and totally looked at her girls again. "Why would you do that?"

She straightened, because instead of giving her better footing, her chest display only seemed to make her more exposed.

"Because sex is overrated," she said. "I'm going to keep my focus on my career once I have one." She moved back to the table with her stuff. "Can't do that on my back."

"Whatever you say." He sat at the keyboard and worked out some bars, saying nothing. Absolutely unaware of what had just happened with her.

She peeked at sound-asleep Harley, then placed photos of her four extremely different short-listed gown options on the table before her.

The one with the lace cape-style sleeves and the fitted bodice with the mermaid tail was probably the correct option for this wedding round. The style would photograph so beautifully. Also, it looked like what the wife of a rock star would select for herself.

"What do you think of this dress?" The style wasn't *her* first choice, but it did scream rocker's wife, so it'd likely be the one he'd pick.

"I think you should wear whatever you want." Pencil between his teeth, he scowled at the music paper he'd scribbled and scratched out. He'd been like this for hours.

"But do you like it?" She stood back and squinted at the photo. She wanted him to like it since it was his event, too. Sure, she liked that it accentuated her breasts without accentuating her ass. But she wasn't entirely sold on the lace. There was a lot of lace.

He glanced up.

She held the photo so he could see better.

"I thought we agreed wedding planning would go smoother without my help?" he said, lifting his eyebrows. "I'm the finance guy, and the show up guy, and the stand where you say guy."

"Maybe I changed my mind, and you can add give-opinion guy to your list?" She made the photo do a little dance across the table. "Do. You. Like. It?"

"Like is a funny word." He sort of made the same yuck face as before when he spoke.

"So you don't?" Huh, she seriously figured this one was the one he'd dig.

He frowned and shook his head. "No, too white."

Said no bride ever.

Okay, she crumpled up the photo and tossed it to the bin. Next option.

Unfortunately, the four choices were all white.

But there was one...

She flipped through Wedding Binder Number One and found the plastic sleeve with the reject images she'd held onto for a future wedding.

Her throat clogged a little at the dress image she'd tucked there. She swallowed.

Not white, this one was crimson red with silver accents, and a sleeveless top that wouldn't look great with her arms. The bodice wouldn't even accent her breasts, they'd be on their own. But the skirt was full on Cinderella with a freaking bustle! And it didn't even look silly because the gown was classic and classy and—

"That one." Knox stood behind her, his breath against the back of her neck, and pointed his index finger at the image.

She sucked in a whole bunch of air. *When did he come over here?*

"It's expensive." She traced her fingertip along the edge of the plastic sleeve.

Honestly, it wasn't more expensive than the other dresses. But this one was just...her...and she didn't want to be herself at this wedding because she should be the persona of Irina. The woman Knox married for the photo shoot and the one who married a rock star for the career boost.

This dress was not for that character.

"You've got my credit card." He pointed at the image. "I want that one."

"No negotiation?"

He sighed. "Do you really want the other one? Because when you look at that one"—he pointed to the red dress again and wiggled his fingers like they were tracing stars falling—"you get all dreamy."

"I don't get dreamy." She put on a decidedly not-dreamy mask.

"Dreamy looks good on you." Knox gave her a look that made butterflies flutter.

Yes, this was that look guys get right before a girl leans in for a lip-lock. Their breaths both came uneven, and her pulse sped up. The air between them stilled like all the fizz had left the club soda, but it wasn't a disappointment, because in the stillness something more potent seemed to build.

Harley fussed in her sleep, breaking the moment. They both turned to check on her, but she settled again without them.

Irina took the interruption as an opportunity to scoot away a few inches.

Uh, that thing with Knox—this thing with him—was a no go, because she definitely needed platonic in this shebang.

She huffed, then said, "You're not supposed to think it looks good on me."

"I can think what I want, it's my brain."

She gestured between them. "This gig between us requires that you not notice if I get dreamy or not dreamy."

He held up his hands. "Fine. You do you, boo."

She would do exactly that, thank you. At least, she'd do a version of that—a version that made more sense for the character she'd be playing.

"Have you given any thought to honeymoon locations?" Knox asked. "I was thinking someplace tropical."

Ew. No. "That's a little cliche, isn't it?"

"Things are cliche for a reason."

He wasn't wrong, but—

"We should do something different." She thought about that. "Unexpected."

Something that would get them more attention than doing the usual…

"We could rent a cabin up in Estes Park?" she suggested.

He wrinkled his nose. "With the bugs?"

"I was thinking it's unique, and then we can pop into town often for paparazzi photos. Boom. Rocker and actress not doing the usual same ol', same ol'."

He shook his head. "The problem with a cabin in the mountains is it doesn't come with a tropical beach."

Grr. "Maybe you should just let me handle specifics and you just show up and smile."

"If there are bugs, then I want them to come with white sand and a Mai Tai. Otherwise, whatever you want works fine." He strode back to the keyboard and went back to tapping out the melody of the new song.

No bugs, white beach, ugh.

This was going to be harder than she'd thought. She pulled the red dress photo from the binder and folded it before dropping it into the waste bin. Long ago she'd decided that her life wasn't about red dresses, white beaches, or prickly tingling brought on by her groom. Not at all.

Chapter Two
KNOX

THE PAPARAZZI TOOK the engagement bait like he and Irina were an honest to goodness couple. This was great, because now he had photographers setting up shop in the bushes out in front of his house, but also bad, because he had to talk to his parents to tell them about the wedding.

"Are you *sure* you want to get married?" Dad asked, not buying it for a second. "I didn't sleep the entire time I was married to your mother. The woman took all the blankets— and that was even before the divorce. So I have to ask once more, are you certain?"

"Uh-huh," Knox said, dropping the curtain he'd been looking from behind to be sure none of the photogs stomped on his shrubs. The acknowledgement to his dad was not a lie, because he used more of a grunt than anything.

He held his cell against his ear with his shoulder, and continued to mostly ignore his dad. Not totally, because he was his dad, and that would be rude.

Honestly? Knox didn't want to get married, not really. Marriage was for the marrying type and that was not him.

He was more of the few-night stand type. Nothing too serious to interrupt him long term, but nothing too short, because that would require even more work. He was a fan of cutting corners on all things relationship, just enough to keep life easy.

The marriage brand of messiness didn't belong in his life, not when he had a band he wanted to nurture and a house to renovate. (A fucking house that needed to be finished already.) He didn't cut corners on those two things. Not anymore.

Not after he'd nearly lost the band and realized what really mattered in his life.

He swallowed a lump, because he *had* cut corners with his band, and it *had* nearly ruined the group. The guys were more than a band.

These men were his family. He didn't have strong family bonds outside of them, and he wasn't willing to risk losing them again.

His dad jabbered on about the multitude of complaints he'd had in his own marriage. Knox kept one ear on the conversation in case Dad asked a question that would require a response, and his eye on the room at large. He'd set up shop today on the smelly pink carpet of his soon-to-be living room. He'd bought the house because the bones were decent, yes, but mostly because of location. The end of the cul-de-sac where his bandmates also bought houses made sense for him to call home. Now he only had to wait for renovations to finish so he could actually move in.

The carpet was behind because of some ordering snafu, so they'd been working on everything else before it arrived. Then they'd paint. Then the new carpet would be installed.

Then his home would no longer smell like piss, and, bonus, it would not be the pink color of stomach relief medication, either.

After Irina had fully taken over the other room at Bax's place, Knox had relocated here. With all the wedding bliss up in his grill, ignoring it was getting harder and harder.

It wasn't like he minded bunking with Bax and Courtney…and Irina. But there were too many people in that house and, while he liked people, sometimes he didn't. During those times, he preferred to hide out for a while and do his own thing. Walk around naked, binge some television, order fried chicken and Crumbl cookies.

There were way too many exposed nails in his current project of a home to do anything naked, but he'd bought a television and a beanbag chair to get him through the rest.

Besides, even with the pink carpet in place, the stainless-steel kitchen appliances were nearly out of the boxes, and the place *was* coming together.

"Did you really invite Beatrice?" Dad asked. This time, he paused, awaiting Knox's response.

He sighed, sat in the beanbag, and grabbed his guitar. "Yes, I invited Mom."

"You know I can't be in the same room with that woman." Dad sighed heavier than Knox.

Meanwhile, Knox's stomach churned, because he hated this part. The part where he negotiated a truce between the parents long enough for him to do something important: graduate high school, open for a big-deal reunion tour as a twenty-something nobody, and, you know, get married. Only his publicist, bandmates, their plus-ones, and his manager knew about the reality of the situation. He'd definitely be keeping even his parents in the dark, since they were essentially props for him to convince the world this was a love match. A guy didn't get married to the woman he pretended to care about without the parents present. It just wasn't done. Or so Courtney and Irina both said.

"You can sit on opposite sides of the chapel," he said. "It'll be like you're both not even there." He hoped he could convince Irina to put them in the nosebleed seats at the… shit…where were they getting married?

She'd mentioned it. Yes, she'd mentioned it.

For sure, she'd told him. He'd even given his agreement.

But where had she said?

Crap.

He should find that out so he could check to ensure that the space held plenty of room for him to put between his parents, because God forbid they had to look at each other for one more second of their existences.

"I'm trusting you on this, Jeremy," Dad said in that tone of his that he used when he needed Knox to do his dirty work, buy him a new car, or a house, or that one time he'd sent Knox the bill for his trip to Florence. A trip with many, many, many issues and even more requests for upgrades due to the inconveniences of the five-star hotels.

"I got you, Dad." He ignored that pulling nag in his core that he always got when he made promises like this, because next it would be his mom and the negotiations would start all over.

Irina sauntered into the room with a big-ass grin on her face, and just like that, the day looked brighter. Damn, he liked his bride. Irina was a kick and a half to be around.

"Bride's here. Gotta jet." He said his goodbyes as Irina sauntered through the room from the back door, checking out the latest work of the construction crew.

Her hair color changed as often as her eye color. Though, lately, she'd stuck with blonde hair, but he'd seen her through red, black, brown, and even a blue phase. Her body had the kind of curves that made a man like Knox take notice.

Her hips swayed in the *Little House on the Prairie* dress that everyone in Hollywood wore these days. He didn't really get the whole thing with the 1980s vomiting up their old inventory, but Irina worked that dress in a way that made him actually want to go to a prairie with her. The heels, the chunky jewelry, the way she hiked up one side of the skirt, so it was sort of slit, but not a slit.

He didn't mean to, but he totally licked his lips.

"What?" Irina rubbed at her mouth with her forefinger. "Do I have lipstick everywhere?"

"No," he said way too loudly. He re-centered himself because he wasn't supposed to think his not-for-real bride was sexy. "You're good."

She grinned. "You're so weird."

"Uh-huh." He did the confirmation, but not quite thing again.

"What brings you to Casa de Knox?" he asked. "Do you want to go out front and make a scene for the paps with me?"

"Rain check on the photo op, because since the big engagement news drop, I have *new* news." Irina did a dance with her shoulders.

"Oh, yeah?" He set aside his guitar and cell and stood. "The press has decided I'm awesome again?"

"Even better." Her blue eyes sparkled. Yesterday, they'd been green. Once, she'd even used colored contacts to turn them purple.

He never knew what he was going to get with her day by day.

"Better than that?" Because he couldn't think of much better than that.

"My agent called," she announced. "I. Got. A. Callback." Irina said the last bit with a touch of shrill and a sound he'd never heard come out of her before. "It's not even really a callback because I didn't get the original audition. But they called my agent and got a copy of one of my audition reels and now I've got a callback." She squeed. "A callback, Knox. It's a callback." She bounced on her toes.

"That's, uh…." Great? Fabulous? Sounds good?

"Don't you see?" She stepped toward him and placed her hands on his shoulders, giving him a bit of a shake. "Our plan is already working."

He didn't respond, not quickly. She put her hands on his

cheeks and squeezed them together, so he probably looked like a fish. "It's working."

"But I'm still an asshole?" he confirmed through fish lips, just to get a better idea of what was working and what wasn't.

"Knox." Her words were soft, and her tone was not shrill, not at all. "It's working." Her voice cracked and her eyes got a little misty. "You won't be an asshole much longer."

He reached to move her hands from his face, so his cheeks wouldn't end up frozen like this, but when he got to her wrists, she moved her hands and gripped his. He, uh, felt something there.

Wasn't entirely sure what that was.

Not sexual. Not desire.

But not friendship either.

Huh.

Since she gripped his hands in hers and his thumbs were right there at her wrists, he gave her a subtle graze of skin on skin with the pads of his thumbs.

Okay, there was the sexual tension, because her eyes softened, and she inhaled quickly. So did he.

They stared at each other for a beat, and he had no idea what was allowed. He wasn't totally opposed to banging his fiancée, because he liked Irina. He liked sex and perhaps it made sense to cut out all the nondisclosure bullshit and just get it on together.

He should find the right time to mention that without it sounding like he was a genuine douche canoe.

Before he could form a word about conjugal visits, she stepped back.

He released her and didn't like it one bit.

She ran her fingers in the side ponytail that dropped over her left shoulder. "It's actually working. This could be it for me. For you. For both of us."

He liked that for her. Liked the excitement and the hope in her expression.

"Let's wait to announce it as a win until I'm not the asshole." He'd need to have a chat with publicist Courtney to determine how they could make this engagement work more in his favor, more quickly.

"You may be an asshole, but you're my asshole." Irina said this with a gigantic grin. "This whole thing is bananas. Why didn't I think to do this years ago?"

The answer to that was simple… "You didn't know me years ago."

"Right, but I knew Courtney and she could've arranged for a marriage between me and anyone."

While this was the truth, why did it sting that she just tossed it out there like it wasn't a reflection of him personally?

"I'm glad I'm so necessary." He said it on a grumble and strode into the kitchen area, where he'd dropped a six-pack of Fat Tire when he came over.

While there wasn't a fridge, he set the beer in the corner where the refrigerator would go. Eventually. Soon. When the renovations were completed.

"Oh-ho-ho, no." Irina scooted after him. "Now that our master plan is working, you can't get all mopey. Because mopey is only two steps away from backing out. And you, sir, may not back out."

"I'm sure Courtney could fix you up with someone else." He popped the top and offered Irina the first bottle. "If I get too mopey."

She took it, took a gulp. "I can't switch to Tanner now. Your name's already all over everything."

Why did it bug him so badly when she invoked the name of Tanner?

He couldn't really say why, other than it did. Problem was, she knew this, and she manipulated the hell out of it. He needed to nip that straight in the bud.

Snagging his phone and thumbing through apps, he navigated to the websites he rarely visited. The ones that trashed him on the regular.

Their engagement was top-of-the-page news. He did a quick scan—

Who's Irina?

Irina and the Beast?

Why Knox?

"Ha. That's cute," he said, but he didn't like the flavor left on his tongue, that's why he rarely visited these sites. He frowned, ready to dive into the rabbit hole of shame.

"Okey dokey." Irina moved behind him and looked over his arm. "So let's close that down and move on to things that aren't so depressing."

He turned, stuck his phone in his pocket. "Like what you need from me?"

She pinched her lips and somehow smiled at the same time. "I'm going to L.A. for the auditions. Can you hold things down here and finish up a few of the last tasks?"

What things? "Like wedding shit?"

She nodded eagerly.

"You sure?" He kicked back against the wall, since he didn't have a recliner to lounge in and only one beanbag chair. "My job description was pretty much to show up. Do you really want to trust me with this?"

This is where having an American Express card came in handy.

"Don't worry, I wrote it all down." She held up her cell and clicked a button.

His phone vibrated in his pocket with a clear incoming text.

"Sent." She grinned. "Wedding planner is on standby and it's only a few executive decisions while I'm away, so we don't get behind."

"One question." He held up one finger.

She quirked an eyebrow. The woman had solid control over her facial muscles. He dug that about her.

"Where are we getting married?" he asked, since that was the thing he needed to know most at the moment.

"What do you mean? Where?" she asked, as though he'd stumbled over his word choices.

"Where's the location of our nuptials?" He ran his thumbnail under the bottom edge of the beer label.

She set her beer down on the sub-counter. "Dude."

"Dude, what?" He lifted his hands wide.

She rolled her eyes. "I told you where we're getting married. I asked you if it worked for you and we agreed on it."

He pulled his lips to the side. "Yeah, I'm sorry. I guess I missed it."

They weren't even married yet, and he had a track record of nodding along with whatever she wanted.

She crossed her arms. "Dude."

The tips of his ears itched like they did when he was about to get in trouble. "Why do you keep saying that?"

"I guess you'll have to work harder to remember." She leaned in, scented like cinnamon, tea, and warmth. Could warmth be a scent? Huh. He'd never really thought much about it before, but it was totally Irina. He liked this about her, this comforting bit.

"Or you could tell me?" He turned on his own warmth, the one that usually worked to get him what he wanted. The low tone of his words, soft rasp as they came out of his mouth. Long stare into the eyes of the woman who would be his wife.

She stared right back.

Neither of them blinked.

No one moved.

"Are we having a staring contest?" he asked, shifting so his body was closer to hers. "Because I will win."

"Okay, prove it." She hadn't blinked. Even so, her eyebrows seemed to raise in a dare.

The air between them snapped with awareness.

Then she blinked, snapped her fingers in front of his face, so he blinked, too. "I'm sorry, honey pie, I don't have time to play right now."

She turned on her heel and headed to the back door.

"You're just going to leave me here all by myself?" he asked.

"Do the things on the list, 'kay?" She pulled the door open and didn't even glance behind as she left.

Left without telling him where the hell they were getting married.

Chapter Three

IRINA

BEING SUCCESSFUL WAS EXHAUSTING, and it tasted perpetually like paste.

Worse than that? She missed Denver, all her friends, Harley, and Knox.

Irina slogged down the hallway to her Los Angeles apartment three weeks after leaving Denver, two weeks after a last-minute switch for the next George Clooney movie that netted her a very nice role in a gazillion-dollar production, and a couple of weeks until she said, "I do" to Knox.

She didn't like how much she missed him. Missed how he always made her smile when they were in the same space. Missed how he knew what to say to make things better. Lately, her days were too packed for any effective communication. Her part in this production involved about three hours in the makeup chair every morning to turn her into the best friend for an alien rom-com meets Pitch Perfect. Thank *gawd* she only had a few more days of that torture and then things could go back to some kind of normal.

She pulled a bit of the glue from her hairline—the stuff was in every-freaking-thing.

Uh-huh. That's the part they offered when she'd come to

town for the callback-not-a-callback audition. Now, she entertained multiple new auditions every day. Because of all that, trying to remember to eat, keeping up with the wedding plans, and sometimes getting sleep…she stuck around in California and drowned in an ever-growing list of things to do.

But tonight, things were changing. Tonight, before she fell asleep, she had a date with her bathtub, a Hershey bar, and maybe she'd find ten minutes to catch up with Knox.

That thought had her smiling after a day of forcing all the happiness to show.

She slid her key in the lock and had barely turned the bolt when the door across the hall opened. One would not think this was odd, given that she lived in an apartment building with lots of other people, but that was Courtney's old apartment. The landlord hadn't been willing to let her out of her lease, so she continued paying for the space until the end of the year.

All that to say, no one lived there now.

A glance over her shoulder and she choked a little on her spit.

As if she'd called him into existence, Knox stood there in the doorway of Courtney's apartment with only a white towel around his waist.

Her gaze landed on his chest…tanned with an athletic build that she did not expect from a man who enjoyed macaroni and cheese as often as he did.

Fun fact? Knox manscaped. He manscaped *well* and with attention to detail. That little drop of water trailing over his pecs to his nipple was not playing Plinko *at all* with any stray hairs. She gulped and her fingers itched to help it along the path toward his—

He cleared his throat.

She shook away her temporary fatigued infatuation with his pectorals and lifted her gaze to meet his.

"How are you here?" she asked, because anything else

that might've come out of her mouth would've been inappropriate and involved commenting about his manscaping.

"Airplane," he replied, checking her out sort of like she'd just done to him.

What was she supposed to do with that? They should not be checking each other out, any more than she should be missing him.

"Quick question, while I've got you." He held up his quick-question fingertip. "Where are we getting married?"

She huffed a chuckle. So much had happened over the past few weeks that she'd totally forgotten she hadn't told him. Or, rather, not told him a second time.

Right, so she may be practically sleepwalking to her apartment, but that right there was *funny*.

"No one's told you?" She sort of figured someone would've spilled the beans by now. C'mon with the wedding so close, surely someone had told him?

"Everyone's lips are sealed because, apparently, this is humorous. Me losing my brains here, baby cakes, is hysterical." He shoved his hands at his waist. "I don't see why this is so funny. If I don't know where to be, then I can't show up. Then you'll have to marry Tanner and explain *that* to TMZ."

He'd started talking with his hands, and the guy should be more careful with flinging his hands around like that or he would lose the towel pretty quick.

Then again, she could find out exactly how good he was at manscaping—

"You'll be there. Don't worry." She wasn't feeling very saucy, but she still gave him a wry smile she hoped held a teeny-tiny punch.

"You're not going to tell me?"

She shook her head. "Not until you put on some clothes."

"On it. Get dressed, too, Sweet Potato. Have I got plans for you? Yes, yes, I do." He pointed to her before slinking back into Courtney's apartment and closing the door.

He was here and he was Knox and she was here and…

Alone in the fluorescent lighting of the hallway, she stared at the closed door. One beat. Two. Her eyelids got heavier. Her feet seemed to be stuck in place on light blue carpet tiles. Maybe she could just lean against the chipped white paint of the doorframe for a minute. The residual glue would probably hold her in place until morning.

She shook her head before she actually fell asleep standing up.

Knox could have all the plans in the world, but she had a four a.m. call time tomorrow, only a handful of hours to memorize her lines, confirm with the florist via email, and try to catch enough sleep that she didn't pass out at the studio. Being a grown-up was not fun at all tonight.

Instead of getting swankied up to go out with Knox, she scrubbed at the leftover adhesive, and pulled on her cuddliest pajamas—the pink ones with the cute boy shorts and matching slippers. Then she put on a pot of coffee so she didn't fall asleep mid-memorization. Maybe she could lean against the wall and close her eyes just long enough for the coffee to drip? Yes, this was a good plan, she decided, as the numbness of sleep had already started taking over and she was drifting in a world of Knox and white towels and showers…

The wall pressed against her cheek as fatigue dragged her along. Someone was knocking on the door, calling her name, but she didn't want to wake up. Sleep mattered more than anything else.

"Irina?" Knox called. He knocked again.

She peeled her eyelids open. *Knox!*

Grabbing her script, she sauntered across the small room to the door, checked the peephole—yup, Knox—and opened it.

"Hi," she said, not allowing her gaze to roam any further than a cursory glance.

"Uh," Knox said from the doorway. "We've got plans, Scooby Doo Lou Who."

"I have plans." Sadly, she held up the script. "I can pencil *you* in a couple weeks from now?"

He frowned and strode into the room. "We're getting married a couple weeks from now."

"Yup." She didn't want to admit that he looked good, actually. Not that he was ever woof, but tonight he'd put on slacks and a button-up shirt. He'd even combed his hair and sprayed cologne. If the scented air wafting around him was any sign.

Her one-bedroom apartment wasn't very large, but it was in a nicer neighborhood and had a kick-ass huge window all along one side. She took the cut to her space in order that she didn't have to worry about her car getting keyed overnight, and her mother popped in to use the natural light for her artwork whenever she needed—which was all the time.

Knox started to lift the corner of the sheet Irina had draped over Mom's latest.

"You don't want to do that," she said, hurrying toward him and smoothing the sheet. "Mom's an artist and you will find nothing under there but bad dreams."

Bad dreams and a landscape made up of nude models.

Knox lifted his eyebrows in question but moved away from the art—thank goodness.

Even without nude landscapes, her place was eclectic. All of the furniture came from the secondhand store, but she'd been careful to buy higher-quality pieces with no stains or broken springs under the couch cushions. Sure, none of the colors went together, but she sort of felt like the mishmash of swatches had become her personal stamp on decorating. Like her personal decorating style was I-give-no-fucks but somehow it works.

"I can't go out and play tonight," she admitted. "I have lines to learn."

"I flew out to spend time with my fiancée, Chicka Boom." He pouted, crossed his arms.

"We should've talked first, so you didn't waste your time coming all the way here." She sauntered to the counter, setting the script there. This sucked, she would way rather be out spending time with Knox than here memorizing an alien language that clearly didn't exist.

"I called." He tightened his arms. "Several times, actually."

"Really?" Not that she hadn't been checking her calls regularly, but if they weren't from her agent or a wedding vendor, they ended up in the voicemail pit.

"Courtney tried, too, and because you didn't answer, and she has a teething infant, I volunteered to come out here with Mach and Tanner to ensure you are still among the living." He scanned her from head to toe. "I'm not convinced you're among the living right now."

He came all the way to California to check in on her? Her whole heart softened because that was…sweet.

"You look about ready to pass out." He studied her.

"You have no idea." She dropped her forehead to the pale-yellow tile squares on the counter, allowing the cool ceramic to soothe her for an instant before popping back to life.

"I think I might have an idea." He unbuttoned his cuffs, sauntered into her space, and rolled up his sleeves. "When's the last time you ate?"

"Lunch." That was around noon. Now it was around nine. It wasn't like it'd been that long in between meals. "Where are Mach and Tanner?"

"They headed out to meet up with friends. Last I checked." Without missing a beat, Knox found her pantry. Not that it was hidden, but he had to open the door. He pushed past her stash of Cup o' Noodles and unloaded pasta and a jar of marinara sauce from the depths. "We were going to catch up with them, but I guess I'm cooking for you, instead. This way I can confirm you are not dead status, and you do what you need to do."

Actually, someone cooking for her sounded nice.

"Shouldn't you ask before you just barge in?" she asked, but her heart wasn't in it.

"Uh…" He glanced from the jar of sauce to her. "I could."

"But you're not going to?" Him making her a meal was super sweet, and she appreciated it, but she couldn't just let anyone other than her mother walk all over her into her apartment without even so much as asking first.

"But you might say no," he said, his eyebrows drawing together.

She nodded. "That's definitely a risk."

"Yeah." He shook his head. "I'm going to do this my way instead."

Was he always this adorably smug like that, or was she simply wicked tired?

The cupboard doors opened and closed, and he sang one of the Dimefront songs under his breath while he searched out whatever he needed. Probably a pan, but she was too invested in her memorization and staying awake to glance up.

Still, a little nagging tugged at her belly, because she owed him, and he was being kind.

"Thank you," she said, looking up. "Really, thank you."

"For ensuring you continue to breathe or fixing your supper?" he asked offhandedly.

That got her attention. She said softly, "Both?"

"Fair enough." He continued to move around the kitchen like it wasn't a big deal and, dammit all, she really liked the guy. "And you're welcome," he added.

She made it through the pages and used a plethora of mnemonic devices she'd cultivated over the years, so the lines would stay put for at least another day. Maybe longer, depending on how many hours of sleep she got that night.

Who knew how long she'd been working when she finally came to the last line? Time was funny with memorization. She glanced up from the pages and Knox stood by the stove, fiddling with his phone.

"Hungry yet?" he asked, still looking at his screen. Apparently, he had some kind of sixth sense to know she'd glanced his way.

She nodded, testing out that sense once more.

"Dinner?" He shoved his phone in his pocket and did a talk-show style pose to illustrate the pasta was ready.

"Thank you. Yes." Her stomach was definitely twitchy with the scents of garlic and pasta that invaded her home. She rubbed her cheeks, stood and moved to the pantry, where she pulled out two Hershey bars, handing one to Knox. "I've been waiting all day for this, so I'm thinking dessert before dinner? My reward is your reward tonight."

The plastic packaging peeled away easily so she could break off a chunk from her bar. She let it settle on her tongue and melt there, closing her eyes to experience the full effect of cocoa bean and milk and sugar against her taste buds.

She opened her eyelids, slowly. Letting the experience or the ritual be what it should be. One did not just eat chocolate, it was a full sensory experience, as far as she was concerned.

"I didn't think you liked chocolate." Knox's words were gentle and felt sort of…intimate.

He plated up dinner instead of diving right into his candy.

"I love chocolate. It's my favorite." Her second favorite being peaches and cream, and her third favorite being salted caramel with vanilla.

"Then why are we having strawberry shortcake at the big par-tay?" he asked, sliding her plate across the counter to her.

Look at Knox being domestic, he'd even added a fork.

She set aside the rest of the chocolate bar to save for real after-dinner dessert and rolled the linguine onto the tines of her fork. Why were they having shortcake? "I figured short-cake made more sense for a rock star wedding."

He grimaced. "Why the hell would you think that?"

"I did my research. It was Hendrix's favorite."

"Good for him, but I don't really like strawberry short-cake." He pulled a face.

"When I asked you, you said it was"—she made air quotes with her fingers—"fine."

He fixed his own plate, ignored her air quotes. "I said *that* because I thought *you* liked strawberry shortcake."

Eh. She shook her head. "It's tolerable. I thought *you* liked it."

"The strawberry cake costs thousands of dollars and neither of us even likes it?" He gave her a look like she was a bat shy of a baseball game.

"At least it's gorgeous and a work of art, even if it doesn't taste good." Maybe at her second wedding she'd get a cake that tasted as good as it looked. This wasn't that. This was about appearances and she'd accepted it.

"Can't we switch it to chocolate?" he asked, sort of like a guy trying to get into a popular nightclub, but worried he was out of his league. Which was silly, because she'd totally rather have chocolate, appearances be damned.

"If I make chocolate happen, can we keep the outside the same? You good with that?" She seriously liked the idea of the way they would intertwine the buttercream roses with real roses and strawberries.

"Huh." His eyebrows drew together as he noshed on his noodles.

"Huh, what?" she asked, before lifting her fork to her mouth.

"Just that it's good to know when my fiancée gets sleepy, she's easier to negotiate with." The way he said this, with the deep rumble he rarely used, made it sort of sound dirty.

Which was bananas, and the way her body kept responding to him had to stop because they didn't have that kind of marriage coming to them.

"Your fiancée just really loves chocolate."

"And she wants to make me happy."

"Well, that too." She smiled, lifted her fork to her mouth, and that's when the world quit spinning. Because what the hell had he done to this pasta? Her taste buds were full-on Hallelujah chorusing over this sauce.

"It's good, yeah?" Knox asked, clearly pleased with himself.

She took a second bite. Then a third. "It's from a jar but it doesn't taste like a jar. What did you do?"

"I don't like jar sauce." He pursed his lips. "So I fixed it."

"I've been sitting here the whole time. You didn't leave, and Medochetti's didn't deliver."

"Nope. This is all Knox magic." He grinned, adorably—pride and happiness and…goofy.

"How'd you learn to do this?" She decided not to inhale the pasta and, instead, allow it to have its own ritual. Because it was just that good. Way better than the microwave noodles she'd planned.

"MyTube?" He shrugged. "It's how I learn everything."

When Courtney had first been pregnant with the baby, Irina and Knox had viewed an abundance of MyTube videos on labor and delivery to ensure it prepared them if the baby came during their watch. That had been his idea, and it hadn't been a bad one. They both knew a good amount about baby delivery and the mechanics of how that worked. Thankfully, they hadn't had to put that knowledge to use.

"I'm impressed." She closed her eyes and let the flavors marry against her tongue. "This is so good."

"Irina?" He said her name with that rumbly goodness.

"Uh-huh." Seriously, how did he do this to jarred sauce? Straight-up magical.

"Where are we getting hitched?" Knox asked in the middle of her enjoyment extravaganza.

She peeled open her eyes.

He lifted another bite, but said nothing else.

"I'm going to answer that," she said, because he really should know, and also, he'd more than earned it with the pasta.

Still, she didn't answer right away because the sauce deserved to be savored.

"I'm awaiting your answer," he said, seriously.

The silence surrounded them like an itchy wool blanket—not super comfortable, but it had a purpose and it'd do in a pinch.

He raised his eyebrows.

"I didn't say *when* I'm answering." She doubled down. "I'm taking the time to give the sauce the attention it deserves."

"Irina…"

"Can we agree in the future to listen to each other the first time?" Not such a big ask in the entire scheme of things, and she really struggled when she didn't feel heard. "I'll pinky swear to it, too."

He nodded. "Agreed. But this is one of my two compromises in the marriage. I figure we each get two."

She rolled her eyes with an overdramatic flair. "Your backyard, silly."

"My backyard?" He frowned. "Then my parents will know where I live."

He said this as though it were a bad thing.

They hadn't dissected their family dynamics yet, which was a good thing, because wait until he got a load of her folks. They were hella fun, but a helluva handful, too.

"Yes, your backyard," she confirmed. "Renovations are complete, yes?"

"Paint and new not-pink carpet are going in this week," he confirmed with a subtle nod.

"There is room for a tent, and there's no overhead foliage to prevent the helicopters from buzzing the ceremony." She and Courtney had come up with this plan. A solid plan.

"We're gonna have helicopters?" He had the nope-don't-like-that look again.

That was the point of the whole thing, wasn't it? "We're going to tip off the paparazzi, so they swing by right in time for the big kissy-face kiss."

He had clearly not heard anything she said the first time.

He slurped a noodle. Oddly, it wasn't annoying. "Oh, yeah. We gotta do that, huh?"

Did his lip curl as he said that? She took offense to that on behalf of her ability to kiss, and kiss well.

"Uh-huh. You think you can handle it, or do you need to watch a few how-to videos?" The friendly sarcasm was clear, but with her level of tired she came in half a beat behind.

He made a sound that came out as a *pf-shaw*. "I already know how to do that."

She pulled in a breath through her teeth. "I don't know, Knox." Playing with fire was a bad idea, sure, but she was tired, and it looked like fun. "You might get a refresher before the wedding. I'm sure there are people you can pay for lessons."

He scowled, clearly appalled. "Maybe *you* need a refresher."

"I'm practically a professional!" Well, she was. She was an actress. She'd even gone to performing arts school, and her entire education had been about putting on a show for everyone to believe. Kissing was no different, as far as she could tell.

"You're a professional kisser?" Knox didn't seem to buy it.

Honestly, she was questioning the assertion, too.

"I'm an actress." She shoved her hands on her hips, inhaled deeply. "Kissing is just acting, but with spit."

His scowl deepened. "Who have you been kissing? Because they're not doing it right."

She'd entertain his logic for just this one teeny-tiny second. "How do you figure?"

"I will not address the spit part, because when done correctly, no one is thinking about spit. My point is, kissing is *not* acting." His eyes darkened just a touch, not enough to make her squirm, but enough to make her consider taking a step backwards. "Next you'll be telling me sex is acting, too," he said.

Well…in her experience, it was. She must've shown this in her face somehow, because he tossed his hands up. "I cannot believe my future wife thinks kissing and sex are so…" The forehead lines deepened along his brow. "…mechanical."

Well, they were. Sort of like taking a walk, one foot in front of the other, working toward a conclusion. Eventually, boom, you're there.

"Let's do it." He rubbed his hands together and that square jaw of his was rather appealing. "Come at me. I'll show you."

The low way he said those last words shifted her sex drive from neutral to drive, because her mouth was dry and her lips were tingly and he was so Knox…

She blinked, freaking hard. "No."

Did she say that to him or to her body? She couldn't be certain.

"Why not?" He seemed to genuinely not understand *why not.*

"Because…" There was a whole slew of reasons rattling around her brain. Number one was… Wait, why couldn't they?

There really was not a solid reason she couldn't kiss him. Maybe if she kissed him, her sex drive could chill out when he was around. She could show herself that there wasn't anything special about kissing this man over any others. Then he'd see that the mechanics were simply one step, then the next. Boom. Kiss complete.

A dress rehearsal for the nuptials and a reminder to her body that he was just another guy.

Then, when they were through, maybe, just maybe, she could enjoy the rest of her Hershey bar in bathtub peace.

Chapter Four

KNOX

LIFE WAS OFTEN CONFUSING for Knox, and more than once he'd questioned the way he operated as a human in a world of rock 'n roll and all that entailed.

The one thing he'd never—*not once*—questioned?

Whether kissing a woman was a step-by-step "how to" mechanical project. Because every kiss was unique, different. Each pairing initiated different feelings and no two times were ever the same.

Call him a connoisseur, but he enjoyed kissing, and touching, and enjoying a woman while she, in turn, enjoyed him.

Don't even get him started on sex, because even the bad sex he'd had in his time was still *good*.

"Fine." Irina stood and stomped in his direction. "Kiss me. Then we can finish eating. Then I can go to bed."

He studied her. Was she serious?

She was serious.

Since she was serious, apparently, she'd never had someone kiss her like he meant it. Which was bananas, because she was a gorgeous woman with a fantastic personality and a pair of lips he wasn't ashamed to have fantasized about occasionally. Not in a skeevy way, just the way a guy notices a woman has kissable lips. Like he noticed she had good hair and a pretty smile.

"Are we gonna do this?" she asked, and was that a little wobble in her voice? Dare he say she was nervous? Probably because she was about to get her very first breath-stealing kiss, courtesy of him.

So, yeah, yes, uh-huh, they were doing this.

He nodded, and ran his tongue over his top lip, deciding the best way to go about giving Irina her first real kiss. He'd give her the kind of kiss that would make her toes curl and her heels kick.

Unless.

He scowled the moment it hit him—*he was being fucked with.*

Ah, hell, she had to be screwing with him. He pinched his lips together like he'd sucked on a lemon-lime sour candy.

"The faces you are making are not encouraging." She said this with her usual spunk, but there was still that undercurrent of nervous energy coming from her.

The two of them hadn't spent an enormous amount of time together, but they had spent a good chunk. During the last Dimefront mini tour, she'd ended up on the bus with him, Tanner, and Mach. The four of them watched birth videos, drank beer, and bonded.

Irina was a first-rate actress, but he'd been around her enough to see any cracks in her facade. Right now? Not one crack.

Damn him to hell, she was fucking serious with this bull-shit and not screwing with him.

Which meant…he was on.

Stopping about a foot away from him, she raised her eyebrows and made her eyes big in a *well* motion. She gave a good show, but the way the pulse in her neck thrummed a quick beat gave her away.

Oh, yes, they were going to do this.

Except what the hell was in her hair?

"You've got a little…" He gestured to his own hairline.

"Yeah, it's glue." She brushed at it. "From costuming."

He could work with a little glue, he'd done way kinkier than that.

Setting his fork down beside his plate with intention, he lined it up with the side of the table, took a small swallow of water, and reached for his chocolate bar. With an ease he wasn't particularly feeling, he kept eye contact with her as he cracked open the seal and removed a small square of candy.

Irina said nothing as he did all of this, but she continued watching his motions as he moved. Today her eyes were a slate gray with little blue flecks. Of all the eye colors she wore, this might be his favorite.

He stood, pushed his chair in, and held the edge of the chocolate to her mouth. Quizzical, she parted her lips only enough for him to slip the candy there, the pads of his fingertips brushing against the smooth skin. A little zing of attraction caught him slightly off guard. Her pulse beat quicker, too, and their bodies pulled together by some unseen magnetic force.

Not the time to think about that.

She let the candy settle against her tongue, and his palm found the way to her neck, tilting it so her face slanted up.

The air between them crackled with chemistry as he studied her slate eyes with the little blue flecks around the edges, and the dilated pupils.

Oh yeah. He let the chocolate mix with the scent of her, but he didn't kiss her right away.

That would be expected, and Irina needed a dose of the unexpected to understand this wasn't mechanical at all.

Instead, he leaned in and ran his nose along the edge of hers, the scent of cinnamon, chocolate, and Irina turning him hot. Her body responded to his, even if she was going to deny it later. There was no mistaking the way her mouth parted the slightest bit, and her breasts pressed a little against him.

An actress could pretend all the rest, but she couldn't dilate her eyes on command.

Could she?

No, he was certain.

"Are we doing this, or are we just standing here?" she whispered against his mouth, but while the words were strong, the little crack in her voice gave her away.

She cleared her throat.

"Irina." He tsked. "Relax and enjoy the experience."

He traced his fingertip along the back of her neck, and he was pretty sure her nipples got harder when she pressed against him. Yup, they were harder.

"I was just super hoping I could get some sleep tonight," she went on. "And the pasta's fantastic, and we're just standing here, so—"

He kissed her.

Was it to make her stop talking? Partly.

Also, it was because enough was enough.

She made a small squeak noise when he pulled her tighter against his chest and tilted his head to get better purchase on her mouth. Chocolate, Irina, and this science experiment came together for one exceptional kiss. Probably one of his best, if he was being totally honest, maybe even top-three.

Irina made a sound in the back of her throat as her hands went to his neck and she held on there.

He went with it, his body reacting to hers in a way he was totally on board with.

Top-two kiss, for sure.

Still, he kept control of the experience, so it didn't become one of her mechanical bull rides. Though, given the way their tongues tangled, and the way her body pressed against his, and the noises that came from the back of her throat, there was nothing mechanical about this ride.

Actually, he was enjoying himself pretty fucking well, too.

He took the kiss deeper, sliding his leg between hers when she tried to climb him like an oak. He didn't grip her ass because he was being a jackass. He did it so she didn't fall over, given the way her core pressed against his thigh, and the moans came from her throat.

They should've done this a long time before now. That was the goddamned truth.

Irina's palms moved to where his shirt met the top of his slacks, pulling at the fabric there like she just couldn't get enough.

But if they went that direction, she'd get no sleep. And, while he'd appreciate her willingness to let him have his way, he also didn't want to be a major contributor to her lack of rest.

Gently, he set her back down on the floor, lightened the kiss, and removed his thigh from between her legs. Was he hard as steel while he peppered little kisses against the side of her mouth? Yes, but he'd deal with that later.

Finally, back on even footing, they were both breathing wicked fast.

"What do you think?" he asked with a wink. "Ever had a kiss like that?"

Because he hadn't.

That was a top-shelf make out session, if he said so himself. Judging by the way her puffy lips pressed closed and then open, she was still finding her way down from the peak. Hell, he was blinking hard himself and a touch wobbly.

Good for him, he still had it. Though he resisted the urge to blow on his knuckles and rub them against his collar, since that would take things too far.

He caught the moment she slid into character—the character of Irina. This ought to be good.

"Scale of one to ten?" she asked, tilting her head to the side.

Uh, they could do that, if that's what she wanted to do.

"Sure," he agreed, cautiously.

"I'd say you get a solid eight for the creativity points the chocolate brought. Nice work, because even if the kiss was shit—and I'm not saying it was—you know you'd net a solid five just for that touch," she said, totally wrecking his moment of enjoyment.

His lips felt funny, like they were frowning.

"Excuse me?" Character Irina or not, he begged to fucking differ.

He stared at her, because apparently she'd grown another head while he'd kissed the hell out of her.

"The kiss itself was super nice." She nodded as she spoke, even counting off on her fingers. "Definitely one of the better first kisses I've ever had. So I'd say you get a solid seven for that."

Was she doing drugs during the day? Was that what the problem was? Because there was no way anyone would ever have described that kiss as "super nice."

"If I were to give it a ranking, I'd think I'd go seven-point-five, leaning into the seven-point-six territory." She grinned and patted his arm. "Don't worry, I bet next time you'll do much better. The first kiss is always the worst, amiright?"

She dropped back into her chair and went to town on the pasta like the world hadn't just shifted underneath them.

He didn't move because he couldn't bring himself to get past the idea that this woman, the woman he was going to marry, had given him a seven-point-five on their first kiss. A first kiss where she nearly came on his leg, and he'd made her pasta.

A seven-point-five wouldn't even take him to the finals of the Tonsil Town Olympics. Hell, he wouldn't even make the team. He'd end up on the amateur tour, and that was unacceptable.

"There was not one thing wrong with that kiss." Why did he sound so defensive?

Oh, right, because there wasn't anything wrong with that kiss.

She beamed up at him, and her eyes got bright before she glanced away again.

Hold up. She was acting now. He'd bet money on it.

"Thank you, you are so sweet," she continued. "You liked it? What do you think? Scale of one to ten for me?"

Wait, was she acting? He made a sound that was not a good one. "You're serious right now?"

"Knox, yeah, this is fun, right?" She grinned huge, but it didn't quite meet her eyes.

You know what? Actually, he wasn't really hungry anymore.

"I think I'm going to…" He tilted his head toward the exit. "Go catch up with Tanner and Mach. Let you…" He waved his fingertips in a circle toward her. "Finish."

Her expression gentled and she pulled her lower lip between her teeth. "I didn't mean to hurt your feelings. I mean, really, first kisses?" She pulled a face.

Yeah, this was not helping his pride situation. Not at all.

"Thanks." He wasn't entirely sure what he was saying thank you for, but he wanted out. Away from there to someplace where his tongue was appreciated for all it could accomplish. "We'll catch up later."

He shoved his hands in his pockets and headed out the door, but he did not go to the apartment. Instead, he called a ride share and tracked down Mach and Tanner where they were partying it up at Pew, the latest and greatest nightclub where everyone wanted to be seen.

He'd planned to take Irina there before the whole pasta and kiss embarrassment.

Pew was the kind of nightclub with strobe lights and aerialists, loud music and good booze. He was Knox of Dime-front, so he'd reserved one of the VIP tables with no issue.

"What's wrong with you?" Tanner asked when Knox nursed his second beer without saying more than a handful of words.

Mach was dancing with a crew of women, but that wasn't Tanner's gig, so he stuck back at the VIP table with Knox.

"You ever kiss a woman?" Knox asked. Because while Tanner was a drummer, good-looking enough guy—so he was told—and he had groupies tossing themselves at him on the regular, he got tongue-tied whenever he was around women under the age of seventy.

"Yeah." Tanner squinted and made a duh face. "I'm awkward. I'm not celibate."

Huh, that was news. Not the awkward, that was well known, but the other part. How did a guy get laid when he couldn't say two words to a woman without clamming up?

"I kissed Irina." Knox admitted it.

A grin stretched across Tanner's face, and he held up his drink for a clink. "Oh yeah. Good for you, kissing your future wife."

Knox met the clink, because he couldn't leave a guy hanging. Unfortunately, he wasn't really feeling it.

"That's the thing," Knox said. "She gave me a seven-point-five."

Knox's foot tapped, because he couldn't seem to get that number out of his brain. The number combo ran on repeat in his skull. *Seven-point-five. Seven-point-five.*

"She rated your kiss?" Tanner lifted one side of his upper lip. "Is that a normal thing for you?"

Not until that night.

"A woman's never rated your kiss before?" Knox asked, because, yes, this was weird.

"Usually, we're doing other things, so ranking our snog session doesn't come up." Tanner made a face like his beer had gone skunky. "Not sure what I'd do if I gave my best effort, and she gave me less than a nine. Did you give your best effort?"

Knox snorted. "Did I give my best effort? Don't I always?"

Tanner held out his hand and made an eh-sometimes gesture.

"One of the best kisses I've ever had," Knox said. Confessed. Whatever.

"Ouch." Tanner glanced around the room. "Maybe try with a lady here? I bet they'll be honest. Maybe Irina was having an off night. Maybe it's not you."

"It's not me, it's her?" That sounded like something Knox would say to one of his buddies to make them feel better, but really, it'd make them feel worse.

"You said it, man." Tanner lifted his shoulder. "Not me."

Knox glanced around the room, but he didn't want to kiss anyone else. He wanted to kiss Irina until she couldn't slide back into that protective character cocoon that had hurt his feelings. His body wanted more of her, not someone else.

"Maybe I picked the wrong wife." He frowned.

Tanner chewed on that thought for a moment. "Last I checked, you didn't pick this one."

"Well, no." Knox frowned. "But I couldn't let *you* marry her."

"If she's tossing out rankings for oral activities, I'm sorta glad to have dodged that one." Tanner took a gulp of his beverage of choice.

Actually, Tanner was on to something.

"That's what we should do." Knox snapped his fingers.

Tanner squinted. "What?"

"You come with me. You kiss her. Then we'll see what she ranks you." Boom. Done.

Maybe if she got a truly terrible kiss, then his would look better.

"You want me to make out with your fiancée?" Tanner asked, obviously not buying it. "How many of those things have you had?" He tilted his forehead to the beer.

This was hard, and Knox was not drunk. "I want her to rank you lower than me."

Tanner grinned a shit-eating grin. "What if she doesn't?"

"Well, that wouldn't happen." Would it? Dammit, it *could* happen, and wouldn't that just be the final blow to his pride-and-ego sandwich?

"Fuck." Knox lifted his bottle to the waitress. "Can I get another?"

"Have you considered that maybe she liked the kiss?" Tanner asked, cautiously, like was handling a live grenade. "And she didn't want to like the kiss, so she gave you a bad score to cover the fact that she was all turned around by it?"

Knox wanted to think that, but— "If she was so turned around by it, then she should've been so turned on she couldn't form a sentence."

"But she's Irina." Tanner said this like it was obvious what he meant.

"And?" Knox understood who it was he'd kissed.

Tanner made a face like he didn't really want to say what he was about to say, but he was going to say it anyway. "Unless she's drunk, you can't really tell if Irina is acting or not, right?"

Well, there was some accuracy to that statement, though Knox thought that he knew her better than the others and had a better read on her ability for deception. All that aside, they had all discovered that once she got slayed, Irina tossed all of her acting skill out the door.

Knox nodded. "So I'm supposed to get her drunk and then kiss her?"

That seemed like a bad idea that would make him not a good guy.

Tanner closed his eyes like he was speaking to a child. "No, that would be wrong."

"You just suggested it."

Tanner spoke slower this time, which was silly because Knox understood everything he said, "What I'm saying is, with Irina you never really know where you stand because she's so good at pretending all the time."

"You think?" That was the most obvious statement of the night.

"She convinced us all she could deliver a baby and then we all watched MyTube videos while she actually figured out where babies come from. That whole time? I never questioned it," Tanner said. "Mach. Bax. No one questioned it."

"I did." This was true, Knox had questioned it.

Tanner wasn't biting. "You did?"

"Yeah, but I heard her talking to Courtney about it, so it wasn't a reflection of her acting ability, more of a reflection of my ability to eavesdrop." Which was pretty good, to be honest.

"I'm just saying." Tanner lifted his hands. "Maybe there's more to this than just a seven-point-five?"

Knox frowned, but Tanner was correct. Because if there was one thing Knox was certain of, that kiss was not nothing.

But he wasn't sure what to do with it being something, either.

He didn't want it to be something. But he didn't want it to be nothing.

The problem was that he couldn't get the taste of her out of his mouth—and not because of the chocolate, either. Because he'd had a taste of Irina, and one sample wasn't enough.

"Hey, boys." A woman who would generally be his type slid into the booth across from him and Tanner. Her friend followed. He recognized her from somewhere…she was definitely Hollywood. "You look kinda lonely over here."

Tanner clammed up, as was usual.

Knox lifted his chin. "Afraid we're in the middle of a private conversation."

"Rain check?" The second lady asked, popping a cherry into her mouth and sucking off the juice.

Usually, he'd appreciate that kind of come-on, but tonight he couldn't quit thinking about how Irina tasted.

"Knox," a guy shouted from two tables over. "You're missing your fiancée." He snapped a picture on his cell.

Knox didn't even have time to smile first.

Dammit, that photo was definitely going to be sold to the highest bidder.

Chapter Five
IRINA

WHENEVER SHE STARTED to think about that kiss, Irina took two deep breaths in, then slowly let them out. That kiss was earthshaking and maddening, because Knox had absolutely proven her wrong. She hadn't realized lip-locks could be like that. Mind-numbing overwhelm from the senses was not something she'd experienced before. Leave it to her to muck it up and feel that way about her future ex-husband.

Her future ex-husband who had no problem moving along to other prospects. Her throat got thick at that thought. The online tabloids had splashed all kinds of photos of him living it up with Tanner and Mach at all the exclusive night spots in Los Angeles.

Best that she understood he was a leopard who wouldn't change his spots over one amazing kiss.

Her phone rang with a video request from Courtney.

This time, she answered, because she hadn't meant to ghost her best friend while she'd been in Los Angeles. Or Knox, or anyone else…life had just been freaking nuts.

"Hey Courtney," she said, flipping the camera on and immediately missing her bestie being in the same room. They needed to remedy that situation as soon as filming wrapped and before all the chaos of the wedding took hold.

"She's alive." Courtney had a flair for dramatics she shared with her now-husband, Bax.

"I'm alive." Irina pulled her legs up under her on the sofa. "Can I see the baby?"

Courtney moved her video camera to show little Harley. They did the chit-chat check-in gig before Bax commandeered the iPad.

He held it to his face, frowning, then pulling it back so the visual was not of his nose hair.

"Seven-point-five?" he asked. "And you're avoiding him?"

Oh shit. She hadn't been avoiding him, she'd just been on set, and he'd been going out with the guys every night. It'd been easy enough to see that the ranking hadn't bothered him *that* much. Not with the amount of partying he'd done in the meantime.

They'd swapped messages, which was evidence she wasn't actually avoiding him, even if she did hole up in her apartment whenever she got home. It wasn't like he'd come knocking or asking for seconds.

"Knox told you what happened," she said, a guilty ache settling in her chest.

"It's all the guys can talk about," Courtney said from off-screen. "All they've talked about for *days*."

Irina pulled her lips together. "I'm glad Knox has someone to discuss it with." What did it say he discussed it at all? "And, no, I'm not avoiding him." Was she? Crap, maybe she was…she didn't mean to, though. "I needed to focus on running my lines for another audition." She held up her notebook where she'd made notes about those lines. *Lies!* "I just…" She couldn't let herself feel those wonderfully distracting things again when they couldn't mean anything. She couldn't let them mean anything.

"You've got shit to do." Bax nodded. "But I'm worried

about my friend. He's taken a hit to his ego over this whole thing and he's—what's that word you used, Courtney?"

"Ruminating," she hollered, again from off-screen. "Becca said when you mull over the same topic over and over with every-freaking-body in the band, it's called ruminating."

Becca was Linx's girl. Linx played bass for Dimefront, and he'd fallen head over heels for Becca. She was a therapist by trade, and her skill set came in handy for the band on more than one occasion. Like now, when they needed to know what ruminating meant.

She and Irina weren't close, but Irina dug the way Becca went with the flow and never shied away from any conflict the band struggled with.

"Knox is ruminating," Bax said, as though this were a really bad thing.

"About the kiss?" Irina did her best to go with nonchalant, I-can't-believe-he's-obsessing. The truth was, however, that she had fudged a scene early in the day when she got overly internally focused on the best lip-lock she'd ever experienced.

"Uh-huh." Bax moved through their Denver house to the kitchen and went about multitasking while talking to Irina and mixing up a baby bottle for Harley. "Guy needs a redo."

Oh, no, no, no. The first kiss was a toe-curling disaster, she didn't need to step in that ring again just to play with fire. Best to just marry the guy, let that run its course, and then file for an amicable divorce without any emotions involved.

"Irina," Knox called from the hallway as he knocked.

"Here's Knox now," she said, cheerfully. "He must've heard me come in."

"Nah," Bax shook his head. "I texted him that you're there and want to talk to him."

Irina smoothed her shirt, hoping she'd gotten most of the glue out of her hair on the drive home, and moved to let Knox in. Tanner and Mach were right behind him.

"You two can come in, too."

"Sweet." Mach held out his knuckles for a bump.

She complied, then did the same for Tanner.

"Bax is trying to convince me you want a do-over on the kissing," Irina said as she moved to the refrigerator to grab beers for the guys.

"She's twisting my words," Bax said from the screen.

"But she's not wrong," Courtney added.

Knox took the offered beer and hooked his hip on the counter, lounging like he was perfectly comfortable and not rehashing their previous kiss fest over and over.

"I have actually, after a good deal of thought, decided to give *you* a second chance," Knox said.

She blinked at him, because she wasn't quite sure what to say to that. "You think I need a do-over?"

"I'll be quick." He stepped forward to her, his eyes sparkling with humor.

Clearly, he was not going to let up on this. She should just do it. Maybe this time it wouldn't be so great and then they could both move on with their wedding plans.

"Okay." She gave a wave toward her lips and held her face up in his direction. "Let's do it."

That got her a wry grin as he moseyed toward her.

The man was not in a hurry, and she sort of wanted to growl at him for that.

Still, she steeled herself for the coming kiss, while ensuring her neutral give-no-fucks expression stayed in place even if her nerve endings danced a jig at the idea of another Knox kiss.

Then she waited, letting her eyelids drift closed in preparation for the onslaught of hormones.

Her heart thu-thudded against her chest, her breaths quickened, and still she waited.

What the heck? She opened her eyes.

He'd moved closer, yes, close enough so he could trace his

finger along her jawline. That touch had all her exposed nerves raring to go for another big event.

Her lips involuntarily parted, the traitors, and she itched all over for a release. Damn, she wanted to kiss him.

Unacceptable. Totally unacceptable.

Also unacceptable was the lack of kissing going on. Not even a chaste peck on the lips.

"Wow," Tanner said, the word drenched in sarcasm. "With all this kissing, I should invest in Oral B stocks."

Bax snort-laughed from the iPad. Courtney did something because he stopped and said, "Ow."

Meanwhile, Knox didn't move, but even in not moving she could taste him, sense him, feel him…everywhere.

She moaned, dammit. She made a noise that was usually on reserve for sexy times and sexy scenes. A sound she'd practiced and practiced, but had never given involuntarily like she just did for Knox.

Knox, who stepped away with a smug smile plastered on his face.

He stepped back to his beer. A beer which he pressed his lips against. Dammit all, she was jealous of a beer bottle and pretty sure the beer bottle moaned too at Knox's touch. The difference? The beer bottle actually got the goods.

She pursed her lips and cleared her throat. Regained her composure and pointed to her mouth. "We doing this?"

Ack, that sounded a teensy bit desperate.

"Nope." Knox wiped at his lip with the back of his hand. "I got what I need." There was that smug smile once more.

"What, precisely, did you get?" Irina asked, because she'd been there and neither of them had gotten anything.

Bax started to speak. "I think I know—"

She gave the screen a look and held up her index finger, hoping she got her point across. That point being that she wanted the info from Knox.

"I just understand that Tanner was correct when he gave

his assessment at the club." Knox grinned a shit-eating grin before taking a pull of his beer without any consideration for what had just gone on with her body.

"What was Tanner right about?" Mach asked. "It's one of the first times for him."

Tanner whacked him on the shoulder. "Uncalled for."

"This wedding is actually going to kill me," she muttered. Or was it the groom who would cause her death? More likely the groom than the wedding. The wedding hadn't made her moan like that. Not once. Irina shook her head and needed an immediate, intravenous infusion of wine.

"Next time it'll be you who kisses me," Knox said, smoldering and proud.

"So…never?" Irina did not love that she was all kinds of turned on and frustrated at the same time.

"Wedding, baby." Knox said this as though she were the only person present.

Tingling tickled her toes, continuing all the way up to her stomach.

"While we're on the topic of the wedding. Can we be groomsmen?" Mach asked, gesturing between him and Tanner. "I've always wanted to stand up at a wedding."

"Yeah, sure." Irina shrugged, but kept her focus on Knox and his unwillingness to follow through with promises his body had made during those moments they'd been close to each other. She was all turned upside down over the not-a-kiss.

"Don't I get to pick who stands up with me?" Knox asked, tilting his head to the side and totally seeing through any bull-shit she was trying to peddle.

"I guess it depends on who you are going to pick?" Irina countered, breathy, way too close to him, and really wishing they weren't having this conversation and instead tangling tongues.

Knox thought on that for a moment, then seemed to come to some sort of conclusion. "I guess you two are in."

"I don't want to stand up at a wedding." Tanner sort of whined and held his hands up in a pose of surrender.

"Too bad." Mach tossed him a beer. "Somebody's got to be sure they go through with it. Might as well be you and me."

Hold up.

"Why wouldn't I go through with it?" Knox asked, even as that exact same question flitted through Irina's brain.

"Same question, but from me." Irina pointed to herself for clarification purposes.

"I'm not worried about Knox. He still needs you," Mach said, taking a swig of beer. "But aside from needing someone to finish up that kiss, *you* don't need *him* anymore." Mach suddenly looked like he'd eaten a chicken bone whole. "Oh shit, you haven't realized that yet, huh?"

What was he talking about?

"Mach? Are you trying to ruin their wedding?" Courtney asked from iPad land.

"'Cause it seems like you're trying to ruin their wedding," Bax continued.

"Realized what, exactly?" Knox asked, but the wheels in Irina's head were already turning.

She had a gig, multiple opportunities for more work, was swimming in auditions, and her agent actually got to negotiate on her behalf—*go her*! Which meant…she didn't really need the inconvenience of a marriage to Knox or his not-kisses to launch her career. Not when it was launching with only an engagement.

Her jaw went a little slack and she stared at Mach for a long moment. The guy was correct, *she* didn't need to marry Knox.

"I think she realized it," Tanner said, but it sounded like he was in a tunnel with the way her brain matter sorted through scenarios of how this could play out with the least amount of effort for her and for Knox.

"Do something, Knox," Bax said, earnestly. "You're losing her."

"Hold up, Chickpea," Knox said, striding back to her with the type of command she'd wanted him to take with that not-a-kiss situation. "Before you go wild and call off the wedding…" He reached for her shoulders, rubbing his hands there.

Dammit, she hated that she wanted him to keep doing that.

"Remember we made a deal," he continued. "My side of the deal has not come through yet. Therefore, by section b, subsection twenty-five, you are *still* legally required to marry me."

"Section b?" Irina asked, scrunching up her nose and trying to make her brain work again because it'd gone blank when he got close. They'd gone all verbal on this thing and there was no talk of subsections. Though there was a prenup in her inbox that Knox's manager had had drawn up to ensure their assets remained separate through the entirety of their sham. She had every intention of signing it once she had a free moment to actually read it.

"I'm just saying that you're getting your cookies early, but mine are still baking." Knox crossed his arms, He had a look of genuine concern that she might ditch him. "Until they finish baking and move to the cooling rack, we see this through."

"I'm not…" She glanced around the room to the guys, then to the iPad where Courtney and Bax held Harley between them. "I didn't say…"

"You didn't really have to," Mach said, examining his now-apparently-super-interesting beer bottle. "We get it, no one actually wants to marry this lug."

Generally, she was an adept enough actress that her standard mask of neutrality was practically adhered with muscle memory, but not tonight. Tonight, she growled.

"Check it out, she just growled at you." Tanner knocked Mach's arm with his elbow.

Now that she'd released it, Irina turned her growl on him.

Oblivious, Knox was frowning as he thumbed through his phone, tapping on the screen as though sending a message. This was good news because they couldn't ruminate on the toe-curling kiss from before or the not-a-kiss from three seconds ago.

They were being totally normal. She was in her cozy apartment, Knox was fiddling with his phone, and Tanner and Mach had stopped giving her shit. The only thing to make it better would be Courtney in the same room.

"Okay." She maneuvered into her kitchen and pulled out a brand-new box of red wine from the cupboard. Cracking the seal, she poured herself a glass. "Here's the deal."

She took a deep drink, trying to think of the best way to say this. *Simple, go with simple.*

"Of course I'm still going to marry Knox." She slipped her gaze to Knox, who glanced up from his phone and stared at her kind of funny, like he'd genuinely been concerned she might bail. "Because he's right, we made a deal and I'm not backing out on that." She wouldn't do that to him.

"Good to hear," he said, but his heart wasn't entirely in it. His forehead scrunched as he went back to his phone, frowning deeper.

The air around him had turned fuzzy and he wasn't his usual happy-go-lucky, MyTube-watching self.

She didn't like that, not one bit.

Chapter Six

KNOX

DAMN. Damn. Dammit. Damn.

Knox stared at his cell like it'd grown a head and spoken directly to him.

"Do you all want to give us a minute?" Irina asked through the fog of have-to-deal-with-this rolling through his mind.

His cell rang and he set it on the table beside the sofa, carefully backing away. It continued to ring with a chirping bird tone he'd programmed for his mother's calls because it was supposed to be calming. He figured if it was calming, maybe he'd want to answer it. Unfortunately for him, all it did was give him a hefty aversion to all things bird.

Vaguely aware that Tanner and Mach had left, and Irina had turned off the video messenger with Bax and Courtney, he couldn't pull his eyes from the birds chirping from his telephone.

She reached for it—

He hopped forward and blocked her before she could swipe it. "Don't do anything. Stay still and maybe it'll stop."

Her pretty pink lips made a cute little oval, but he didn't move. She didn't move. No one moved.

Why was everything warm in Irina's apartment? He scratched at his arms. Hot and itchy and—

"You are panicking." Irina stood right before him—how'd she get there?—and placed her hands on his shoulders. "Why are you panicking?"

There was air moving in and out of his lungs. Of this, he was certain, since he hadn't done a face-plant into the carpet fibers near his still-ringing cell.

The chirping stopped.

He let out a huge breath. See? Totally breathing.

"Thank fuck," he whispered.

"What is up with that?" Irina asked, whispering, too.

He glanced to the phone, then to Irina. "My mom."

"Your mom." Irina's eyebrows raised right up.

He nodded. "She's in town. Wants to meet up. She's going to ask me to do things. Things that I don't want to do."

"Like?"

"Like have a lunch with someone important so she can show me off." Or rip on his dad and try to convince Knox to cut him off. Or many other things he couldn't think of right then, like— "Or convince me not to marry you."

"Then tell her no," Irina said, as though it were only that simple. "Tell her you're going to do what you want to do."

"I can't." He didn't seem to be physically capable of it.

Irina frowned. "Why not?"

"Because she's my mom."

"Instead of telling her no, you're just not going to answer."

He nodded. "Exactly."

The phone started up again.

"Knox." Irina still stood before him, still touched him, still…cared? "She's very persistent."

He closed his eyes, gulped, and let that lump of whatever-it-was settle square in his gut like it always did when he shared the same zip code as his mother.

He glanced to the window, then to the door. Not that Mom would scale the side of the building, but she'd definitely track him down and knock on the door. Not that tracking him down would be that hard with the photographers placed strategically out front of the apartment building.

"I need to leave for Europe now," he decided. "Stay there until the wedding."

That's when he'd planned to see her next and deal with all her drama. Uh-huh, perhaps a trip through the United Kingdom, hop on a train to France. He could already taste the French pastry he'd have as he meandered down the cobbled streets a full earthly rotation away from the woman who lived to make life hard for everyone around her.

"Knox, the wedding is nearly here." Irina rubbed at his arms. "You can't go to Europe."

"We could get married there." He snapped his fingers and appreciated his own quick thinking.

"Knox." She lifted her hands to his cheeks and held his gaze to hers.

This was comfortable, Irina's touch and her eyes on him. Her concern, because she cared that his night was about to go to shit. He could just stay here in her apartment and stare at her. That would be better than listening to his mom go through her list of reasons marriage was a mistake in person instead of via text messages.

He looked away, because he needed to process this change of events. *Think, Jeremy. Think.* He pulled free of Irina's grip.

"Your mom doesn't want us to get married?" Irina asked, gently.

He nodded.

"Then tell her you're going to do it anyway," Irina said.

He paced to the television, stopped, turned. "You don't get it… No one tells my mother no. About anything. I thought I could avoid her until the wedding. Figured the boys could play interference with her and Dad while we did our

thing. Then I—we—can get married in peace and I—we—
can escape before I have to say anything other than, 'Glad
you made it.'" He bit at his knuckles.

His cell started up again.

Maybe he should toss it? But then he'd have to get a new
one and that'd be a whole thing.

Irina picked up the phone with no understanding at all of
the matches she held in her palm, or the fire they could start.

"She's only a person," Irina said.

Irina had no idea. None. Zippo. Zilch.

"That's where you're wrong. I'm not entirely certain she's
human. I think she's mostly bulldog." His mother was a
bulldog who tore apart anything in her path, and Dad was an
old man trapped in a younger body. He lost his filter early on
and said the first thing that came to his brain. Most of the
time this was a bad, bad thing.

"Let's go take her out for a drink on neutral ground,"
Irina suggested like a madwoman seeking to be destroyed.

His cell continued with the chirping.

"Nowhere is neutral when it comes to my mother."
Perhaps he sounded a touch overdramatic, but he'd lived his
whole adult life avoiding her whenever he could. Sure, she
seemed nice enough. But whenever she came around, he
ended up unhappy, and she'd get what she wanted. That's
why he avoided her, like the grown-ass man he was.

"You also have parents," he said. In times like this, the
best course was to show the other person how totally wrong
they were, using their own life as example.

She nodded, gestured to the nude in-process statue near
the window. "My folks are eccentric, too. I get it."

He shook his head. "No matter how *eccentric* they are, they
have nothing on the two-person tornado that created me."

Birds kept right on chirping from his phone.

"Can I please answer your phone?" Irina asked, already
reaching for the device.

You know what? If she wanted to play with fire, he might as well let her. She couldn't say he didn't warn her.

"Answer at your own risk." He shivered. "But I wouldn't do it." *Didn't do it. Same difference.*

She held it to him to unlock and then, without the necessary hesitation, Irina lifted the phone to her ear. "Hello? Is this…"

"Yes, this is…" Her eyes went wide. "So nice to finally—" She stopped speaking.

Mom tended to do that to a person.

"…uh…hi…" She made a c'mon motion with her hands to Knox.

Call him dense, but he wasn't sure what that meant and he wasn't about to get involved in the conversation.

"You're my future mother-in-law so I call you…" She tossed a panicked look to Knox.

What the hell did he know about this type of thing? What did she call her?

"Can I call you Mom or Ms. Dillion?" She gently whacked him with the back of her hand on the biceps. "No, of course I know your name. I understand you didn't use your ex's name because he's a…right. There were substantial differences."

Oh, okay, she wanted to know Mom's name?

He tilted his head a little to the right. Wait…he'd already told her his parents' names when they were doing the invitation. Had she forgotten? Or was she not listening when he spoke?

Well, well, well, pot meet kettle. He crossed his arms like a line in the proverbial sand.

"Of course, Knox talks about you all the time." If it were possible, her eyes got wider.

She must do that when she panic-lied to her future mother-in-law. That was a good thing to note so she'd stop doing it before she actually met Mom. That kind of tell was the type of thing that would get Mom all kinds of riled up.

"Beatrice," he said, letting her off the hook, but they'd be discussing the whole didn't-listen-the-first-time shebang. "She never took Dad's name. Her last name is, and always has been, Connor."

Irina pushed a chunk of hair behind her ear and said with a smooth confidence, "It's Beatrice. Ms. Connor."

She paused. This wasn't good, because that meant his mother was talking. Talking loads.

"Uh-huh." Irina glanced to Knox and frowned. "No, I agree…"

That got him scowling, because there was not one thing his mother could say that he'd like Irina agreeing with.

"It's just that—" Irina chewed at her bottom lip.

He probably just should've kissed her instead of unlocking his cell. Then he'd be the one who got to nip at her lip.

"Yes, there's a prenup." Irina shifted on her feet.

Knox cringed internally.

"I absolutely believe in the union. That's not why we're getting the prenup, we just want to be sure Knox's finances are—" Irina paused. "That's not—" She frowned. "Yes, I understand it's a contract detailing what will happen when the marriage dissolves." Irina's frown deepened. Yup, that's the type of expression his mother put on people. "I'm not sure that's…mm-hmm…" Irina stared vacantly in his direction, blinking hard. "I'll make that work." More blinking. "Yes, of course. I'm looking forward to this. Okay…" Her eyes did the wide thing again. Here came that panic lie in three…two…

"My pie is burning in the oven. I've gotta go." She dropped her chin, but continued holding the phone to her ear. "Apple. Why?" More blinking. "I'm not sure which kinds of apples I used tonight. Whatever they had at the store?" Lots more blinking.

While Irina may have elected to jump into this particular ring, she had no idea the cliff she'd hopped off of, so he slipped the phone from her hand, didn't hold it to his ear as he spoke into the receiver, "Hi Mom. Gotta go. Pie's burning. Bye."

He hung up the phone while the words, 'Told ya,' itched against his taste buds. He didn't say them, though. Didn't say anything.

"We're having breakfast with your mom tomorrow." Irina crossed her arms across her chest. "Some fancy place in Bel Air."

"That is not happening." He shook his head. "Not happening at all."

"I'm not certain how it's not happening, given that I just agreed to it." Irina pulled her lips into a frown.

"Don't you have a call time in the morning or an audition?" he asked.

She shook her head. "We wrapped production and I cleared my day tomorrow to spend it working out wedding and marriage stuff."

"You're about to get the stomach flu. A twenty-four-hour thing, don't worry. I'll go to breakfast and deal with my mom and hope they poison me. It's better this way, since she'd probably talk you out of the wedding, anyway."

"What does your mom do for a living?" Irina asked, carefully.

He didn't talk much about his parents, so he hadn't actually given over the information before. Not like, say, his mother's name. "She's an attorney."

Irina's eyes turned to little slits. "What kind?"

"The kind that always gets her way."

"I mean what branch of law does she practice?" Irina pushed on.

"She's a prosecutor," Knox said. "Federal."

"Wowza." Irina seemed to be reconsidering her decision to agree to the marriage.

He didn't disagree with this reconsideration given the gale-force winds of his mother. Unfortunately, this reconsideration came too late, since they were already elbow deep in this wedding.

"You can't go tomorrow without me." Irina actually seemed remorseful that she'd taken the call, what with the way her toe etched a triangle in the carpeting and her mouth went into her thinking pout. "I'll say no for you. It'll be my job as your fiancée."

"Or you could just hit me in the head with a hammer?" Knox asked. "Then I'll be unconscious." Problem solved.

Irina crossed her arms. "If I knock you out, then who's going to knock me out?"

Fair point.

"Don't worry, I've got your back on this," Irina said in a way that he actually believed her.

He soaked that in—she had his back. His throat got oddly tight at that thought.

"You're going to make an excellent wife." He held her gaze with his, enjoying the feeling of her all wrapped up with him in the moment.

She didn't look away, just allowed that thin thread of connection to remain. The way they seemed to be communicating without saying a word. The way his whole body felt like he'd come home. All of that with just her gaze.

He dug that.

"I'll see you in the morning?" he asked.

"Seven?" Neither of them moved. "Meet here?"

He nodded. "And Baby Cakes? I told you my mother's name when we did the invitation list. Next time you should listen, so I don't have to repeat myself."

Irina's eyelids pressed to slits, but her lips twitched with humor.

"I believe you also owe me a few pies?"

"I've been busy." She tossed her hands to the side. "But I promise I will bake your pies. Pinky swear."

"I was already promised pie. There has been no pie."

"How's my song coming along?" she countered.

"A rain check it'll have to be." He shrugged, because he hadn't started that yet, either.

"Thought so," she said with a wink.

Chapter Seven
IRINA

DRESSED UP, rocking her chunky macrame sandals, and ready to kick the day's ass, Irina paused in the hallway before knocking on the door to Courtney's—Knox's—apartment.

"Irina," her mother's voice called from the end of the hall.

Irina let out a sigh as her mom flowed toward her. "Hi, Mom."

Seriously, she practically flowed, ethereal with her red hair tied up at the top of her head, a massive canvas rolled under her arm, and a twenty-something guy wearing a trench coat following behind. "I thought you and Dad were doing a drive to the Grand Canyon?"

Dad had wanted to take photos there for some contest he planned to enter.

"Plans changed." Mom lifted her hand in a whatcha-gonna-do motion. "Now we're back. You don't mind if I use your light today, do you?"

Technically, no. Irina never minded sharing her light, but today was a different kind of day with Knox. Knox, who may not understand the art happening in that light.

"Who's your friend?" Irina asked.

"This is Brayden." Mom waved her hand toward the model. "Brayden is an art-student-slash-model and I'm giving him a lesson while he poses for me."

"Please tell me Brayden has clothes on?" Irina made big eyes at her mom. The one wild card this day didn't need was a naked guy in her apartment while she met her future husband's mother.

"He's wearing socks *and* a coat." Mom waved her arm toward model guy. "Totally decent."

You know what? Irina didn't have the time to deal with this at the moment, because she needed to chat with Knox.

Waiting until Mom and her model were safely behind her closed apartment door, Irina knocked on Knox's door and waited. Adjusted her sleeves and stepped back and forth in her sandals.

Aside from outfit selection, mornings were not Irina's favorite part of the day. Not by a long shot. The adhesive they'd used in her morning makeup sessions sucked lemon-scented golf balls, but she was certain she'd prefer it to a breakfast with her future mother-in-law.

Lucky for her—

Knox opened the door.

"I got the best news," she said quickly. Not the model or her mom, but real news they could use to their advantage.

"Does it involve coffee?" he asked, moving aside so she could enter. "'Cause the stuff here isn't drinkable."

"It's drinkable," Mach grumbled from the couch. "I'm drinking it."

He was, in fact, drinking a steaming cup as she moved into the room.

While Knox was up and dressed with hair still damp from an apparent shower, Mach was still in his jogger sweatpants—no shirt—and he flipped through his cell while drinking from a coffee mug.

"You're drinking it, but one plus one does not equal two."

Knox had on a black, worn-in, kick-ass Pantera tee and a lived-in pair of blue jeans, with bare feet. "I actually don't know how a person can screw up coffee so consistently."

Mach kept right on flipping through whatever was on the screen of his cell. "I triple filter it."

Knox slipped his gaze to Irina.

Funny, she'd never noticed how she enjoyed the way a Knox look slid against her skin like small touches against each fine hair.

"He means he's too lazy to separate the filters, so he just tosses them in the coffee maker," Knox said, the small touches thing not seeming to register with him at all.

"I think the words you're searching for are 'thank you.'" Mach didn't even glance up.

Knox shoved his hands on his hips. "The words I'm searching for are, 'I need Starbucks.'"

"Down, boys," Irina said, because they were acting like canines about to pee all over each other to prove who was in charge. In the end, all that would make was a mess.

Knox clearly needed an infusion of caffeine before he started his day. Good to know about one's future husband.

"Tanner takes his time," Mach said, voice gruffer than usual since he was also not a morning person. "It'll be a while."

"You made Tanner go get you coffee?" Irina squinted at Knox, because that wasn't very nice. Not at all.

"He was going to go get his own, I asked him to snag one for me." Knox squinted right back at her, mimicking her expression. Poorly, she might add.

Still, her tummy flipped a little because the expression was super adorable on him. She wasn't sure how she felt about getting a little bit of a crush on her fiancé. Getting turned on by his kiss was one thing, but an actual puppy love crush? Was that even allowed in this situation? She'd need to ask Courtney.

"If the barista is a pretty girl, it'll be next month when you get coffee since Tanner won't be able to form a vowel sound. Much less place an order." Mach lifted his mug to his mouth, took a long pull, and made an *ahhhhh* sound before smacking his lips.

The pretty girl thing was Tanner's deal.

Not what one would expect from someone as good looking, young, and mostly confident as Tanner. He didn't get caught up talking to women or bringing them back to his bed.

Nope. He had a hard time forming words around single women under the age of seventy, until he got to know them well. Once he trusted a woman, he stopped looking like a tomato whenever he tried to conjugate a verb around her.

It'd taken him a solid four months with Irina and sometimes he still got a little pink in the cheeks when they chatted.

"If he's not here in ten, I'll go rescue him." Knox sighed, overdramatically.

"You're such a good friend," Mach responded, dryly.

"Coffee. Check. Irina, you have news?" Knox asked, turning back to her.

"Yes. I do." She smoothed the waist area of where her red and orange paisley blouse tucked into her teal jeans. "As I was saying when I arrived, I have excellent news."

"But it's not drinkable coffee," Mach said from the sofa.

Knox hopped up on a barstool, his neanderthal feet hooked against the footrest. "Whatcha got? Because both of our days are about to go to shit over mediocre crepes with my mom."

Nope. Their days were just fine. A-okay and perhaps even awesome.

"One of the actresses in the Templeton Production Residency had an emergency tonsillectomy," Irina said, doing her best to broadcast her sympathy, while also being excited about her opportunity.

Knox stared at her funny. Even Mach gave her some side-eye.

"She's fine," Irina assured. "But she's not going to be talking or singing for the next three months." She sort of sang that last little bit.

"That sounds horrible." Knox's expression turned pained. "I had mine out when I was thirteen. It was worse than Mach's coffee."

Mach opened his mouth. Probably to defend the honor of his coffee, but they didn't need to go backward—

"You're right. It is. Totally horrible surgery for her." Irina sauntered to the kitchen to pour herself a cuppa and see what the fuss was all about. "But thanks to her faulty tonsils, we don't have to meet with your mom now." She flashed a pair of jazz hands before serving herself up some coffee with a dollop of creamer.

"I have no idea how one of these things has to do with the other?" Knox scratched at the back of his neck. "Can you draw me a visual dot-to-dot?"

Mach snorted.

"This means we are flying to Denver today!" Irina said, poking her finger in the air like she was actually completing a puzzle.

"Uh. Why?" Knox didn't do that math, but that was her fault, because she hadn't exactly been clear with her word salad solution.

"Because I have an audition for the part." She lifted her mug to her lips, took a small sip through her massive grin. "Immediately."

There was nothing wrong with that coffee.

"Serious?" Knox asked, a slow grin spreading.

Irina grinned right back. "Your mom can't make us meet with her when we're five states away. Ba da boom."

"You know she'll talk us out of going." Knox frowned. "She's that good at what she does."

"That's why we're not calling her until we're in the air." Irina held the steaming mug closer, going for her best villainess impression. "By then, it'll be too late."

"It's remarkably frightening how you do that so easily," Mach said, dryly.

The door pushed open, and Tanner strode through with a carrier of Starbucks cups. "Coffee's here."

"Already have some." Mach lifted his mug. "So does Irina."

"I got you a vanilla latte." Tanner handed over a Grande size cup for her.

Oh, she was going vanilla latte for sure. There wasn't anything wrong with Mach's coffee, but if there was a vanilla latte in the room, with her name on it, there wasn't much right, either.

"You're the sweetest." Irina took the offered coffee, set her mug in the sink, and reveled in her good luck of the day. Everything came up Irina.

"When's your audition?" Knox asked.

Tanner beamed and held out his knuckles. "You got another audition? Awesome."

This audition was such a big deal. She loved all things acting—theater, film, television—all of it. While film had been her goal because the paychecks were so much heftier, she kept a super soft spot in her heart for theater productions.

She nodded. "Theater. Denver. Leaving in about an hour for the airport."

"I thought you wanted to do movies?" Knox asked, taking the offered cup from Tanner, and completing an elaborate handshake with him without ever breaking the thread of attention he'd placed on Irina.

"I want to act." And get paid well for it. "Wherever that may be." There was something to be said about performing for a live audience and the thrill that came from that rush of energy they shared with the performers. She didn't want to be stuck only on film or television—she and her agent agreed she wanted to do it all.

The excitement of not knowing what would happen next or if someone might fall off script and a girl would have to go rogue. Not to mention this production of *Love Me Tonight* was, honestly, one of her favorite plays of all time. She knew the soundtrack by heart, and she wasn't ashamed to admit that sometimes, late at night, she'd dream about being cast in the role of Persephone.

Now she actually had the chance, because Persephone number one was about to need an understudy.

"Honestly, getting engaged to you has been one of my best decisions," Irina admitted without even a shred of doubt.

"So far I'm still waiting for it to work out for me," Knox grumbled, even though he hadn't been slayed in the tabloids for a whole forty-eight hours.

Irina draped her hand over his shoulders like she'd done dozens of times as his platonic friend. This time, however, the side of her breast perked to attention where it met his shoulder. Her body's reaction to him was getting silly.

She dropped her arm and pulled off the top to the vanilla latte, because she hated drinking goodness like this through the teeny little hole. "I wonder what's going to happen once we get married. Maybe my career will really take off."

Knox was giving her a funny, quizzical look. Maybe the side boob thing had affected him, too?

Nah, the guy had seen and felt loads of side boob, she was certain.

She placed the lid on the counter next to his cup.

"What are you doing?" Knox asked, nudging the lid with the tip of his finger.

"Fancy coffee tastes so much better when a girl can get the full mouth experience," Irina announced.

"The full mouth experience?" Mach asked.

"See, you can get a better gulp. Like this." Irina illustrated, opened her mouth wide and pulled the foamed milk through her lips using the precise amount of suction, so the vanilla-flavored espresso cooled before hitting her taste buds.

Mach slid his gaze to Knox. "You have the potential to be a very lucky man, you know that?"

Tanner turned tomato-sauce red.

"What?" Irina asked, mentally scrolling back to the last time a guy had had the opportunity to appreciate her abilities with latte foam. Then she stopped that because she hadn't done that since—well, not since she'd decided to focus on her career and forgo any new attempts at trying for love.

"I guess we should pack." Knox smacked his knees and stood. "You boys heading back or are you staying put?"

"Heading back," Tanner said at the same time Mach announced, "Staying put."

"I guess I'm staying put because somebody's gotta keep an eye on this one." Tanner jerked his thumb toward Mach. "I'll head back in a few days once he's got Los Angeles out of his system."

"I guess this makes it easier to ensure they make it back on time for the wedding." Tanner lifted his cup, but he left the lid on.

The man had no idea what he was missing.

"You're supposed to ensure we get back in time?" Knox asked, his eyebrows scrunching together.

"Duh," Mach said.

"Why else would we come?" Tanner pulled up the barstool next to Mach.

"Because I am an awesome mentor as you enter your rock star adolescence?" Knox asked.

Did he seem disappointed? He totally did.

That disappointment made her chest ache a little, which was not acceptable when she had an excellent fancy coffee, and she didn't have to hang out with her new mother-in-law and listen to Knox complain about the crepes.

"Can I get a 'woot woot'?!" Irina did a shimmy shake. "We don't have to have crappy crepes today. We're going to Colorado."

"I kind of want a crappy crepe, now," Mach said. "But I'll settle for Knox to leave the rest of his cookie delivery here from last night."

"You got cookies?" Irina sniffed. She hadn't smelled any cookies when she'd arrived.

"Fridge," Tanner said. "Grab me a chocolate chip, yeah?"

Irina moved to the refrigerator and opened the door. There were lots and lots of cookies there. Boxes and boxes of Insomnia cookies. Mach did not lie.

"Did you buy *all* the cookies in the greater Los Angeles area?" She turned her gaze to Knox.

He slowly lifted his gaze from her ass, up, up, up her body to meet her glance.

"I don't believe in doing anything halfway," he said, and the way he said it? She felt the need to slurp some vanilla latte.

"I beg to differ." Mach pulled himself from the sofa, stretched, and…huh…he didn't manscape at all. He had a good deal of hair on his chest. Funny, she used to think she didn't have an opinion. But, now, she realized she totally preferred a manscaped chest.

Good knowledge for the future, after this marriage, if she decided to actually date someone again. That was going on the checklist.

Knox shrugged. "When it comes to cookies, I go all in. I take my cookies seriously."

Then he sipped his coffee through the plastic lid—like Tanner—without even giving the full mouthfeel experience a chance.

"Knox, I know you're in there, open the door." A female voice, a voice she recognized from last night's phone call, came clear as a bell through the metal-plated apartment door.

The knocking, however, was not on this door. The knocking was on Irina's door.

Shit. Shit. Shit.

"No, no, no, no, no…" Irina bolted to the door and flung it open.

Too late.

The meeting of the moms was happening right there in the doorway of Irina's apartment with Brayden in his socks.

Chapter Eight

KNOX

KNOX WANTED to use his body to block the gap so Mom couldn't just strut on through without getting past him first, but Irina made it to the hallway before him, right into the line of fire.

He never enjoyed the staring-directly-into-the-headlights-of-an-oncoming-semi experience of his mother's arrival.

He also had no idea how to make it stop. His neurons seemed to quit firing, his limbs wouldn't move, and his blood pressure knocked into panic territory.

Today was a special kind of traffic accident because there was a naked guy wearing only socks and a fairly transparent sheet, a woman who sort of looked like Irina, and his mother, all crowded there together.

"Jeremy?" Mom took in the entire situation, looked to him, and then she cleared her throat. Mom was her usual self —makeup and hair that came from some salon, and a navy blue business suit with flat dress shoes that poked from the hem of her slacks.

. . .

HE MADE the mistake of stepping into the hallway to be closer to Irina, which made room for Mach and Tanner to join them.

"Uh. I feel like I missed something?" Tanner asked. A legit query, seeing as everyone was rooted in place.

"This is Knox's mom." Irina tilted her head in Knox's direction. "And my mom." She gestured to her mother. "And Brayden."

Who was Brayden and where were his clothes and why was he in Irina's apartment?

"I'm going to do anything else other than *this*." Tanner took his three cookies, his coffee, and headed to the bathroom.

"You're going to eat cookies in the bathroom?" Irina asked through the door to him, appalled. Which, in any other circumstance, would be funny.

Clearly she hadn't spent enough time on the road with them, because that was one of the more uninteresting locations to enjoy pastry.

Tanner took half a bite of one cookie. "Yup."

"I'm out, too." Mach slipped off to the bedroom, which left Knox and Irina and—

"Mom, this is Knox. And Knox's mom," Irina said, like all of this was absolutely normal. "How great we all get to meet before the big event!"

Knox raised his eyebrows, because surely Irina understood by now that cheerful optimism wasn't going to help her out with his mother. She was more of a persistent bumblebee with unlimited stingers that distributed just enough toxin to get you to bend to her will, but not enough to stop your breathing.

Mom was likely evaluating who got the stinger first, since usually she didn't have such a wide variety of options.

"Mom." He managed to say her name with the appropriate reverence to make her happy, and even added a touch of glad-to-see-you to the tone. "I thought we were meeting at the restaurant?"

At least that's what she was supposed to think.

"Change of plans." She adjusted the chain of her purse against her shoulder.

Unless she had the ability to read minds, or she had staff listening in on Irina's phone, there was no way for her to know that plans had changed. Which meant—

"I've got to head back to San Francisco straight away, and then up to Tacoma." Mom flashed him a peroxide smile. "I was stopping to take a rain check on breakfast, but this is all very interesting." She gestured to the look-alike Irina and dude in a sheet.

"Big case?" Knox asked, unsure what to say about the rest of the happenings in the hallway.

"You have no idea," she murmured. "This is Irina's mother?"

"Janis." Irina's mom held her hand out to his mom to shake. "We're working on an art project." She winked at Brayden. Then she moved in for a Knox hug. "Knox, it's so great to have you as part of our family. We are going to have so much fun together."

"Oh," Mom said, and for the first time in forever his mom was flustered. "Beatrice," she said her name a little too late.

Janis already worked to usher the guy back into Irina's apartment. "We better get back to it."

"Shall we go inside?" his mom asked, rubbing her hands together as though she didn't quite know what to do with them.

"You know, Mom, if you're working a big case, it's okay if you can't make the wedding." He tried, really tried, to sound sad that she might skip.

"We need her," Irina stage-whispered beside him.

But, did they? Did they really? Because if she didn't show, his day would be that much easier. While, yes, the photo op would be better with her, there was less chance of a bar brawl style ending if she and his dad didn't both show.

"I was very much hoping to convince you and Irina to postpone." Mom started to push into the room, but he held firm.

"Uh." This is where he said no, like Irina suggested.

"We want to get married." Irina looped her arm with Knox's. "We're going to get married."

"Why?" Mom asked.

Well, one, because Irina worked hard on the wedding. Two, because he hadn't gotten his end of the bargain yet. (That morning the tabloids had trashed him with photos that were nearly two years old!) And three, maybe he was finally ready to do what he wanted.

Childish? Maybe.

True? Yes.

"Are you going to invite me in so we can discuss this?" she asked. "Or do I have to wilt out here in the hallway?"

"Inside is good." Irina had moved behind him, her chest to his back—which, he'd noted, didn't suck—and she rested her chin against his biceps. "It's so great to meet you in person, Bernice."

"Beatrice," Mom corrected, giving Irina a solid once-over. "You can call me Ms. Connor."

This wasn't going well.

"Wonderful. I forget things when I get nervous." Irina made a goofy face like a cartoon character.

Impressive, and sort of cute.

He grinned at her. She grinned at him.

Mom, however, cleared her throat and was *not* grinning. "May I come inside?"

"Of course." Irina stepped backward, pulling Knox by his favorite Pantera shirt. The one he wore when he needed to remember that he was a rock star, goddammit. A successful one, at that. And he didn't need his mother's approval to marry a woman he planned to divorce in a year. He didn't. She didn't even need to show up. Except for photos.

Otherwise, totally unnecessary.

Irina wound herself around his arm, totally playing up the part of doting fiancée.

The shit of it? He liked it. Liked the touching, the way her lips grazed over his shoulder and her eyes sparkled when she looked at him. If he didn't know she was acting, he'd totally buy that she was into him.

While his head fought the war over the legitimacy of her attention, his body didn't seem to know the difference between reality and pretend. The way his ears buzzed with awareness and his lips tingled with the hope of a kiss? His body did not care if it was pretend or not.

"Would you like a cookie or something?" Irina asked.

"Not pie?" Mom asked, dryly.

Irina made an expression that looked like blah. Seriously, how did she do that?

"Burned," she said. "But we have cookies?"

"I hope you don't mind, I looked up your address." Mom dug through her purse on the counter, then clipped it closed without removing anything.

"I do."

Mom lifted an eyebrow. "I figured dropping in would be so much easier than attempting negotiations for a quick meeting, but I don't know where we are at the moment if you live across the hall?"

Irina sighed. "My best friend has this apartment, but she's in Denver and it's—long story. The boys are staying here."

"Knox too?" Mom asked, going in for the interrogation.

Knox pulled Irina close to his side. "Save the questions, yeah?"

Mom paused at his request.

"You're not sleeping in the same bed?" Mom pushed, recovering quickly.

Irina did the wide eyes thing she did right before she lied through her teeth, which was a bad idea because this was his mother, and she was the queen of figuring out lies. Best to go with the truth.

"Knox's bandmates are staying here while they're in town." Not a lie, good job. "And my mom is an artist. She prefers the lighting in my apartment for certain projects, so we decided to pop over here."

"So we were chatting with the guys," Knox tacked on. "But they scattered to give us privacy when you arrived."

He needed their asses to show he wasn't a Fibber McFibberton. "Mach, Tanner, come meet my mom, *Beatrice.*"

Irina snorted a little, and kissed his shoulder with adoration. Adoration and a heavy helping of teeth.

Nice. He liked the teeth.

"Hey." Mach sauntered from the room, this time wearing a shirt, *thank fuck.* "I'm Mach." He held his hand out to Mom. She shook it. "Pleasure."

Tanner didn't show. But that worked because Mach played excellent interference, totally distracting his mom with way too much charisma. Though, give the guy credit for taking on the task. *Mach for the win.*

"You should kiss me," Irina said against Knox's earlobe. "Make it look good. But no tongue in front of your mom."

"So on a scale of one to ten, you'd like a two?" He figured he should just confirm this before he wrecked his score without reason.

"Knox." Irina wound herself around his arm, not inappropriate, just as though she were comfortable enough in his presence to touch him like this.

Honestly, he liked the touching. Appreciated it, and wanted more.

He wasn't supposed to enjoy it enough to want more.

"I can't kiss you. You're supposed to kiss me. Remember? Rules." He'd laid down the line that she'd be the one to kiss him so he couldn't back out on that now. Of course that had to happen before his mother entered the picture.

"Kiss me already, stud," Irina whispered against his ear, gripping his forearm with her fingernails.

Fine. Whatever. She didn't have to ask him twice. She'd asked him, so that was basically the same as her kissing him.

He leaned in and gave a little peck to her lips. The kind of kiss that two people who truly knew each other would give—a quick, totally-appropriate-for-public-consumption tap against Irina's mouth.

"When she's looking, goober," she said against his lips. "She's not looking."

He glanced to his mom and Mach. Mach was chatting her up with entirely too much charm, he'd need to put a lid on that. But his distraction technique was phenomenal, so he'd definitely go on the wedding rotation to keep his parents occupied.

Mom glanced over. Knox looked down to Irina and she looked up at him. They were way too close, way too startled, and way too out of practice, because first their noses collided, then their teeth.

"Ow." She jerked away, rubbing her front teeth.

He also jerked away, but he added a solid f-bomb to the mix.

Mom frowned.

Mach looked at them like, what-the-fuck?

"Wedding nerves," Irina said, tapping on her front teeth and then running her tongue over them.

They were fine. His were fine.

Their egos could use a touch of hand holding, however.

"You two are seriously doing this?" Mom asked, folding her hands in front of her since putting them on her hips would be way too cliche for her. "Because you could simply live together and not do the paperwork associated with it."

Knox deflated as though she'd stuck him with a pin.

"There are much better ways to make a point to your mother than tying yourself up legally to a woman you barely know."

Hold up. She thought he was doing this to make a point with her?

"What point do you think I'm trying to make?" he asked, because seriously all he was doing was trying to clean up his tabloid image.

"Don't think I don't understand. I understand better than you'll ever know. Marrying a woman you don't love to stick it to your divorced parents."

"Why don't you think I love her?" He scowled.

He did love Irina, even if he wasn't in love with her. He loved the way her smile made him all warm inside and the way she made him laugh.

"Knox, there is no way you'd fall for a woman like Irina…" She scraped her gaze over Irina's eclectic clothing and footwear choices.

Enough was enough.

"This woman—Irina—*will be* my wife. Right now she's my fiancée and she deserves a lot more respect than what you're giving her."

Irina looked up at him with a reverent respect that made him feel ten feet tall.

"Can you please start acting like an adult?" Mom asked. "What can you possibly want from her that you can't get by simply living together?"

Well, now she was actively trying to piss him off.

"You may not accept us, but that doesn't change anything. Yes, she's a major pie tease. She promises pie and then doesn't deliver."

Irina made a strangled sound.

"And, sure, *sometimes* she tastes like glue. Also, when I text her, my phone autocorrects her name to Urine. I don't know why." He looked to Irina, held her gaze with his. "But the wedding is *on*."

"Are you done?" Irina asked, eyes super wide.

With her? Not by a long shot. With his mother? Yeah.

"Learn to accept her as part of my package, or don't bother with any future attempts at manipulating me, because I'll be checked out." He drew a deep breath and wished for a beer. "I mean it, this is important to me. Support us, or don't. I don't care anymore. But if you don't, you can expect a holiday card and that's it. Your call, the ball is now in your court." He crossed his arms.

He'd never stood up to his mom like that before. The whole thing was...different. A little thrilling, but also scary. Scary because Mom stared at him as though he'd grown an extra ear, and his eyeballs had turned purple.

Maybe he should've tested these waters before diving right in.

"You're serious?" she asked in a tone he couldn't recall her ever using before.

Irina slugged him gently on the arm. "I don't always taste like glue."

"Not anymore, obviously. But when you were doing hair and makeup and coming home after." He made a *sorta* face.

"You aren't exactly Mr. Spectacular," Irina huffed. "Your hair is too long, and you smell like lumber."

"You like longer hair, and I *know* you don't mind the smell of my woodsy cologne." Knox crossed his arms.

She'd said she liked it when they were on tour. Said he could probably pick up a truckload of groupies with the scent. Not that he needed the cologne to pick up groupies. Still...

"Not the point," Irina countered.

"Oh, I know I'm better than a seven-point-five. You may not be ready to admit it, but we both know it's the truth."

"All right." Mom held up her hands. "I've heard enough."

Suddenly, tossing down that line in the sand didn't feel like a win. It seemed like he was stepping forward into an uncertain future by pinning his everything to a woman they both agreed was temporary.

Mom reached into her bag and removed a red velvet jewelry box. "I wore this at my wedding. I'm sure your grandmother would want you to have it for your wedding day… so…here." She passed over the box to Knox.

He opened the velvet box and inside was a gorgeous red-stoned bracelet with silver accents that seriously looked expensive. Not that he knew anything about jewelry, but he could go do some MyTube research and confirm.

"Hello, gorgeous." Irina moved closer to touch the stone.

"It's horrible luck," Knox said, glaring at his mother.

"There's no such thing as luck." Mom shrugged. "But if there is, maybe it'll hurry things along for you two and we can be done with this nonsense."

"That is a massive ruby," Mach added, not getting close, but the thing was big enough he could get a good look all the way across the room.

"Get married, if that's really what you want, but you can't say I didn't warn you." Mom waved at the box like she was glad to be rid of it. "I'll see you at the wedding."

Just like that, she sauntered to the door and let herself out, leaving Knox holding the jewelry box and a lot of questions in her wake.

The first? What did a guy do once he stood up to his mother for the first time in his life?

Apparently, he went home to Denver with his sham of a fiancée.

"Is Tanner still in the bathroom?" Irina asked, frowning at the bathroom door.

"Nope." Tanner pushed open the bathroom door and strode to the living room. "I was just waiting for the scary lady to leave, so she didn't eat my soul."

"She won't eat your soul," Knox said. This was the absolute truth. That would be too messy. "She'll just convince you to eat it yourself."

"He's not wrong." Irina draped her arm across his back, giving him a squeeze.

"You don't have to keep pretending. She's gone," Knox said.

"*Au contraire*." Irina snuggled in deeper. "That little performance we gave illustrates exactly how much we need to rehearse." She rolled up on her toes to press a quick kiss to his lips. Their noses didn't crunch together this time and there were absolutely no teeth crashing.

"Better," he said. "A solid five out of ten."

Irina shook her head, and he couldn't help the grin on his face.

Unfortunately, he had no idea what that meant for their future or their present.

Chapter Nine

IRINA

RUNNING lines at the TSA line was about as awesome as one would think. But they made it through. Knox went exploring, and she drenched herself in all things Persephone.

Gah, she wanted this role. Even for a little while, at least while Persephone number one recovered her voice. Then… maybe…no, she wouldn't think about getting to work on a long-running show.

The self-doubt butterflies flitted in her stomach. Her agent said she wasn't a slam dunk, and there were others in line for the roll. A-list others.

Which only meant she had to kick the audition's ass.

"I never meant to hurt you, Sergio," she spoke to herself, under her breath. "Sergio." She said his name deeper. *No, that doesn't work.* So much needed to be said in that one name. She had to project longing and hope, but understanding that, as Persephone, she'd mucked everything up. "I never meant to hurt you… Sergio."

Yes, that worked better. Long pause before his name. Time to look deep in his eyes and wish she—Persephone— had made different choices.

"We hurt the ones we love most, not because we hate

them, but because they are the ones who see what we can be."
That worked, the lines flowed smoothly. The problem
remained the Sergio line. That's the one she had to nail. The
one word that held the emotion of two and a half hours of
theater, if she did it right.

Perhaps she should choke up a little more? Yes. "More
frog. This line needs more of a croak," she murmured to
herself.

"More frog?" Knox asked, cutting through her attempts at
character creation.

"Mm-hmm." Irina scribbled a note to herself before
glancing up at Knox. "How was the airport?"

"It smells like feet and the bathrooms are disgusting."
Knox held out a Styrofoam takeaway container. "I brought a
present. Something special to wish you good luck on your
audition."

Aw, that was sweet. Or, at least, it had the potential to be
sweet. What was in the container would determine the sweet-
ness level.

She took the box, holding it on her lap. She gave a little
shake. Something thudded against the sides with crinkling.

Knox sat right beside her, arm draped over the back of
her pleather chair in the airline VIP lounge, right up in her
personal space.

Her heart thu-thunked in her chest.

This was part of the show for the world, she got that. Her
body was a trained acting machine. She could pretend better
than nearly anyone, that's all the little heart hitch meant.

But she actually *did* like how his cologne smelled a little
like sawdust and the woods. She expected him to be all blond,
ocean-scented surfer, salt and fresh air.

"Are you gonna open it?" he whispered in her ear,
winding a chunk of her blonde hair around his fingertips.

The little tug echoed lower, between her legs. She shifted.
Down, girl.

She didn't get turned on when doing an acting job, there was no reason to be turned on now.

To distract her from the hair pulling deliciousness, she popped the Styrofoam lid.

There, wrapped in red-checkered wax paper, was a super sad strawberry, banana, and Nutella crepe. Sure, it was probably fine to eat, but it looked like it had seen the bottom of a boot—or an aggressive spatula.

"I dropped it, but the container stayed closed, so the food is fine," he added.

How sweet was he?

"You brought me a crappy crepe!" Bonus, she didn't have to eat it with his scary mother.

His eyes glittered with…was that pride? That was totally pride.

She leaned in and brushed her lips at his cheek. Unfortunately, he turned his head as she moved. She didn't want another nose collision, so she pivoted close and her mouth landed smack against his.

He jolted a little, didn't move, but he didn't move away either.

If they were a real couple, she'd reward him for bringing her a crappy crepe by giving him a serious kiss. The kind that wasn't chaste or a quick peck.

What the hell. This was a show, right?

She parted her lips, moaned a little because it felt right, and deepened the kiss when he went right along with it.

She'd never really enjoyed kissing parts before on set or stage, they were just another thing to do. But this was different.

Another moan and that's all she got to do before Knox took over. Oh boy, did he take over. There was tongue in all the right spots, hands skimming her jawline to places along her neck she did not know were erogenous. She groaned into his mouth, and it wasn't the least bit for show. No, he coaxed that out of her with a substantial amount of skill.

And then…she attempted to sort out what that might mean.

Before she formed even the slightest cohesive thought, he pulled away. Hands clasped behind his head, he kicked back. "Enjoy your crappy crepe, Noodle Cup."

"You don't want to give me a score?" she asked, cautiously.

"Say what you need to say. Think what you need to think." He opened his eyes, stared straight into her soul. "But that second moan wasn't fake, so I know it was a ten for us both."

"How would you know what's real and what isn't? I'm a professional at convincing people to believe what I want them to believe." She'd been through a crapload of workshops, classes, and school to learn her craft.

"Tell yourself whatever you need to tell yourself." He winked. Then closed his eyes. "I know the truth."

She didn't really like that.

But what was it she didn't like?

Did she not like that he was correct? Or was it that he called her out on it? That she wanted more of him and wished the kiss had been real?

Her mouth tasted like sawdust, and not the good Knox scent, either.

Knox sat there with his eyes closed.

She leaned over and brushed her mouth against his cheek. "Knox?"

"Hey." He opened his eyes, meeting her gaze.

"I thought you might want a bite of my crappy crepe." The cellophane wrapper crackled when she removed the red plastic spork with a great deal of flair.

"I'll try anything once." Knox moved back into her

personal space and...actually...she should've let him snooze. Because now she was all upside down again.

Using the edge of the spork, she tried to cut at the crepe. It wasn't budging and the head of the utensil broke clean off. This was ridiculous.

"They really do make them crappy, don't they?" Knox grinned a wicked grin.

Uh-huh. She picked up strawberry with her fingertips, tore off a piece of crepe, wrapped it together and held it to Knox's mouth.

The look of surprise in his eyes was 100 percent worth the broken plasticware.

He parted his lips.

In for a penny, in for a pound. She slipped the bite inside and lingered for a moment in clear invitation for him to close around her fingers.

He didn't disappoint, but he didn't only close around her fingers. Oh no, that would've been too normal. If she'd learned anything, Knox never went with the expected.

He clasped her wrist as he licked residual Nutella from her skin. If he kept that up too much longer, she probably would end up arrested for indecent exposure and illicit sounds.

"Oh, look at that." She pulled her wrist from his grip. "Can you believe it's time to board?"

Close to time.

Same thing.

"We should get going." She did a quick check to ensure she had all her stuff.

Time to move along and get back to Denver without any more licking.

They boarded, settled in their first-class seats—she asked for the aisle because she understood from previous experience that he preferred the window, but he'd never ask for it because he'd figure she wanted it, too. Good news, they settled and everyone kept their mouths to themselves.

He pulled open the window shade and glanced around outside.

She toyed with the Styrofoam clasp.

"You look like you're contemplating the demise of that crepe," he said.

"No." Though she had received actual flatware from the flight attendant, so the guess was solid.

"Then what kinds of questions are bopping around your brain making you look so serious?"

"Why did you call me Noodle Cup?" she asked, still fidgeting with the Styrofoam container.

Why was this the question that popped out of her mouth? She didn't really know, but it was something she'd been tossing around since he'd said it.

"You really want to know?" he asked.

"I wouldn't have asked if I didn't want to know." She shifted so she could dive into the crepe. Even if they screwed up the actual crepe part, they couldn't mess up the Nutella.

"It's sort of a secret," he said.

She leaned closer to him. "Then whisper it."

He moved forward, his lips against her earlobe. The scent of hazelnut, fruit, musk, wood, and rock star.

The scent combination was fabulous.

"I like noodle cups," he said only for her. "You have an abundance of noodle cups in your pantry, so I figure you liked them, too. That's why I called you Noodle Cup."

She didn't shrug off his mouth from being so close to her ear. "That's such a Knox thing to say."

"Well, I am Knox." He kept his mouth right there near her ear.

She liked it.

Liked that he thought of her and brought her a crepe,

liked that he kissed her and sucked her fingers, and liked that he was playful instead of serious.

There was way too much serious in the world to make it part of the daily landscape of her personal life.

"I kind of like the nickname," she admitted. "It feels like us."

Which meant she needed to lock these feelings down tight, because it was one thing to be turned on by him. But there was no way—no way at all—she could allow herself to fall for her fiancé and his cutesy nicknames.

Chapter Ten

IRINA

"SERGIO," she tried, lengthening the vowel sound.

Gah. No. Still not it.

"Excuse me," the flight attendant knelt beside Irina. "We are looking for a physician on the flight. Are either of you a medical doctor?"

Irina shook her head. "I'm sorry—"

"What's the problem?" Knox was all perked-up ears and pent-up energy: a combination that might not end up going well.

"We have a pregnant woman in coach with a situation. You're a doctor?" the flight attendant—Grace, her name tag read Grace—asked.

"Depends on the *situation*." His eyes sparkled, his grin flashed, and Grace was putty in the palm of his hand.

A little green-eyed monster seemed to sit high on Irina's shoulder. Unacceptable, because it wasn't like he was actually flirting. He'd just answered the question.

"He's not." Irina made big eyes at him.

"I could be." He draped his arm around Irina in a claiming movement she didn't quite understand. Then he pressed a kiss to her cheek.

Her body snuggled against him as though they'd practiced this.

"Of the three of us, which one has helped deliver a baby?" Knox raised his hand. "Just me? Okay. Of the three of us, which one completed their emergency childbirth certification course?" He kept his hand raised. "Still just me, huh?"

He did all that? "When did you do all that?"

"I started during the last Rocky Mountain tour. I couldn't actually let you be Courtney's birth guide knowing you hadn't been to any births, so I studied up."

"You watched MyTube," Irina pointed out. "With me." She didn't shift because she liked his arm where it was across her shoulder.

"And then I enrolled in an online class, and now I'm an Emergency Medical Tech." He beamed at this announcement.

"Don't mess around when someone's looking for a doctor." Irina nudged him with her elbow. Then she glanced to Grace, shaking her head.

He couldn't be! That wasn't something a person could just go *do*.

"Look," he sounded as exasperated as she felt. He reached for his wallet and pulled out a red and white card. "I even paid the extra five dollars for a certification card."

She took the card. Seemed legit, but he probably could've made it at Office Depot.

"It's the real deal," he said to Grace. "I can help out if you want. If not, Denver's close, she'll probably make it without issue. Unless, you know, her water broke or something."

"There are no other medical providers." Grace rubbed at her temples. "So I guess it's you."

"What's going on?" he asked, gentle and with great bedside manner.

Arm still draped around Irina, he held Grace's full attention.

"We don't want to alarm anyone," Grace said.

Which, Irina would note, was exactly what a person said right before ringing the alarm bells.

"But the woman's water did break. We're still forty minutes from Denver, so we wanted to see if there's a doctor to help out, just in case. Honestly, you're a real EMT?"

"Real in the sense that I did the training, took the test, and got the card?" He nodded.

"He's a musician," Irina said. Not to blow his cover, but because somebody should probably let them know what he did for a living.

"Dimefront." Grace snapped her fingers. "I knew I knew you."

"When did you have time to do all the EMT training?" Irina asked, because she couldn't help herself. The guy was always writing songs or hanging with his guys.

"It's online. At night." He gave her a when-else-would-I-do-it look.

Well, she didn't keep track of his nighttime activities, but this wasn't what she expected he'd been doing between the hours of ten p.m. and five a.m.

Not that she didn't think Knox was smart enough to be an EMT—he'd proven very apt in the medical emergency area. He even got Courtney to the hospital after diagnosing her with pre-eclampsia in a bar.

She simply didn't know he'd made it official with actual coursework, that's all.

"You know how to deliver a baby?" Grace confirmed. "If we need that?"

"Yeah, I can do it in a pinch. But she shouldn't labor in coach. Can I upgrade her ticket to first class, so I can keep an eye on her?" He gestured to the empty row in front of them.

Irina blinked at her future husband, because that was

even sweeter than the stepped-on crepe he'd brought her at the airport.

Who was this guy and why was she only now letting herself notice?

"This is nuts," Irina said to Grace. "Can't we just land?"

Grace shook her head. "We're close enough to Denver they don't want to divert unless it's absolutely necessary."

One would think a laboring mother would be absolutely necessary. But what did Irina know about planes and landing and schedules?

"I'm going to go get Mom," Grace stood and moved through the curtain to coach. "We'll move her up here."

"I need to stand up." Knox extracted himself from the clinch he'd had with Irina, and started to climb over her. She quickly stood to let him through.

She also moved out of the way as Knox clapped his hands for attention.

"Excuse me," he said to the passengers in their little front of the cabin. "We've got a mom coming up in active labor. Research has shown that fewer people present during labor is actually more beneficial for Mom and baby, so I'm hoping if I offer you all tickets and backstage passes to the Dimefront concert in Denver next month, you might…" He tilted his head toward the curtain. "You know."

"How can you get tickets?" a red-haired lady in the back asked. "Nobody can get tickets."

"Because he's in Dimefront," Irina said. "This is Knox. Keyboard player, sometimes he sings, occasionally he dances."

Little light bulbs seemed to flash over the first-class passengers. Those tickets with the backstage passes were probably worth more than the tickets from LAX to Denver International Airport.

Here's the thing, first class wasn't full, and the six other passengers didn't have to be asked twice. Partly because the

Dimefront show had been sold out moments after the tickets went on sale, and also because laboring Mom showed up and clearly wasn't faking it.

"Give your contact information to Grace, and I'll pass it along to our band manager who will send you passes," Knox said, as they single-filed it back to coach.

The soon-to-be-new mom stopped walking as her abdomen tightened. It visibly tightened.

Damn, Irina had never seen that firsthand and it did not look like it felt good. In the videos she'd watched with Knox, they'd described it as a whole-body hug. But a whole-body hug sounded nice, and that did not look nice.

"It's not a good thing if she can't move through the contractions," Irina said softly to Knox. "She's not talking through them either."

She may not remember a ton of the birth guide stuff, but she did remember that part.

"Yeah." Knox eyed the woman, pulling his bottom lip to his teeth. "I'd say we're entering the transition stage." He held his hand up as he said, "Uh... Grace?"

"Right here." Grace headed toward them from the first-class galley with an oversized first aid kit in one hand and a mobile defibrillator in the other.

"I haven't examined her yet, but..." Knox huddled with Grace and Irina. "I think they should land the plane."

Grace shook her head. "There's no way. There's weather below us, and the pilot's saying it's safest for everyone if we go to Denver."

"Shit," Knox frowned. Then something resolved in him. "Looks like we're doing this."

An odd Cinderella fairy-godfather transformation took hold of him, and he wasn't the keyboardist in a super-famous rock band anymore. He also wasn't the guy marrying the girl for publicity.

He was a man in control of a situation, divvying out orders.

Irina helped make a semi-bed out of one row of first-class seats with blankets and pillows, then did her best to get Mom comfortable even as they hit some serious turbulence and she whacked her forehead against the overhead compartment. Irina, not the pregnant mom.

"You've got extra oxygen?" Knox asked Grace, keeping his voice calm like he was actually in an emergency and knew what to do.

Irina had a solid hope that this was the case, but she also had seen Knox do the splits onstage during the song "Mouthplay." And once he'd left to pee in the middle of Tanner's drum solo.

"Irina." Knox said her name and cut through her memories of him onstage. "Do the birth guide stuff like we practiced for Courtney."

She could do that. It had to be like muscle memory. Somewhere in her brain were instructions for being a birth guide.

Irina hadn't actually had any official birth guide training, but she'd watched enough videos with Knox that she understood how the breathing thing worked. They decided that was probably what a birth guide should focus on. But then Courtney had her baby in the hospital, and she let that knowledge seep out of her brain.

But she did know how to breathe, and count. She did it every day. *I can do this.*

Look, if Knox was certain he could deliver a baby at the other end, she could count and breathe at the top end.

"I'm Irina," she said, bending over the back of the seat, holding Mom's hand through the space between them. "What's your name?"

"Cathy," Mom answered, doing the he-he-hoo breathing thing that Irina had practiced. This was good news because it meant that Mom actually knew more of what she was doing than Irina.

They finished the introductions between a couple of breathing exercises, until a whopper of a contraction took hold and Cathy's face tightened up and turned red.

"You've got to breathe," Irina squeezed her hand back. "In. Out." *Breathe.* "In. Out." *Breathe.* "Baby needs your oxygen."

Birth guiding was like riding a bike, she slipped right back into it.

"How far along is she?" Knox asked the guy who came up with Cathy. "Prenatal care is up to date? How's her blood pressure? Any spots in her vision?"

Irina didn't hear the rest of the answers, keeping her focus on Mom and breathing. Any questions *she* might ask quickly dissolved on her tongue, because Cathy was presently trying to break her fingers with that grasp of hers.

"I think the baby's coming." Cathy adjusted her position. "Like *now.* Right now. Somebody catch my baby."

"Okay. Nobody panic, I know what to do." Knox introduced himself as he gloved up, shared his qualifications— showing his five-dollar EMT card again—and asked if he could remove her pants. He did all of this with a straight face and actual authority. Which was why Cathy and her guy helped Knox get her undressed from the waist down.

Irina had never questioned Knox's ability to get a woman naked, but this timetable had to be a record for even him.

Knox shifted Cathy's hips and a rush of fluid drenched the blanket. This is the part where Irina focused on Cathy's face, because while she may have done an acting job once that involved playing a birth guide, she wasn't really into the whole messy, below-the-waist miracle of birth.

Body fluids as part of any miracle were just not her thing.

Instead, she handled the top-side breathing and reassuring through crushed fingers, while Knox, Craig—turned out he was the daddy—and Grace did whatever they did on the other end.

"You're doing great," she said as Cathy made another attempt at breaking multiple bones in Irina's hand while panting.

And then there was a baby's mewl.

"Congratulations. A little boy," Knox said, holding the baby under the arms and glancing back down between Cathy's legs. "There's just one baby, right?"

"Yes," Cathy said, taking deep breaths and reaching for her son.

"Looks like he's full-term given the vernix situation," Knox said, lifting him to Mom's belly.

Irina couldn't quite move, keeping her focus on Knox with a new little boy. Knox who dealt with the umbilical cord, and rubbed the squirming little person down with a blanket until he started to really wail.

Irina's eyes got teary and not because she had to pretend. There was something seriously special about what she'd just witnessed.

The cabin behind the curtain erupted in applause.

"There's your lungs," Knox said, gently, like the little guy actually understood him.

Maybe he did, because he let out a scream in response that demanded Knox keep talking to him.

He took the cue. "You did a great job. So did your mama. And when you're a teenager, you better be nice to her, because she just pushed you out at like ten thousand feet in the air."

Knox being sweet, her hand being nearly crushed, and that wailing sound? All of it together punched Irina right in the heart. Her throat clogged, her eyes misted more, and Knox lifted the naked, wailing little guy to his mother's arms.

"Welcome to the world," Knox said, in that low, soft tone of his that made Irina want to jump him on the spot.

This man was a serious mystery to her, and she wasn't entirely loving that, because, it turned out, she actually wanted to know everything there was to know about Jeremy Dillion.

"We're approaching Denver. Ready to land now," Grace came behind Knox again. "Ambulance is waiting at the terminal." She glanced to Irina, then to Knox. "How do you want to handle that? We can keep you on the plane until everyone else departs?"

"Why would you do that?" Craig asked. "You should be on the news for what you did. You're a hero."

"Uh, no, I just took a class." Knox scratched at the back of his neck. "I'm not interested in the hero thing. You do it." He smacked Craig on the back.

"You don't know who he is, do you?" Grace asked.

"Uh, Grace." Knox made a nix-it motion across his throat. "Let's not—"

"They're gonna figure it out when they open this week's *People* magazine," Grace said.

"Yeah, let's not talk about that." Knox didn't love the things they'd said about him last week.

"They weren't very nice to him," Irina mouthed.

There'd been more photos from a club he'd visited with Mach and Tanner. He sort of looked like he'd smelled something funny in all the pictures. The tabloids made fun of him.

"Who the hell are you?" Craig asked.

Knox held his hand out. "Jeremy."

"Are you an actor or something?" Cathy asked.

Irina stepped in to say something that might diffuse the situation, but Grace chimed in first, "He plays keyboard for Dimefront."

Craig's jaw slipped open. "Seriously?"

"Let's focus on the important thing, like this little one's name," Knox pulled off his gloves like he'd been on Grey's Anatomy and come out of a particularly gnarly surgery.

"I don't know." Cathy brushed her fingertip across the baby's cheek. "We'd thought we'd name him Sam, but—"

"Awful name, I dated a girl named Sam once." Knox shook his head. "Try something else."

"What about Jeremy?" Craig asked, his arm draped over the other chair to hold the baby's fingers."

Cathy stared at the now sleepy baby. "I like Jeremy."

"I like it, too," Irina said as the plane touched down.

More than she'd ever realized.

Chapter Eleven
KNOX

"IT'S NOT A BIG DEAL," Knox said as the driver merged onto I-70.

"You're right. It's a huge deal." Irina smiled at him from across the bench seat. There was loads of room in the back of the Escalade, and since they'd left the airport and prying eyes, she'd given him space.

He didn't love it.

Didn't love that the adrenaline had worn off of the delivery, leaving room for lots of thoughts to creep in. Linx's wife would probably call them intrusive thoughts, or some shit like that.

Honestly, the baby delivery thing left him a little rattled. There'd been a second when he worried the bleeding wouldn't stop with the afterbirth, and he'd be responsible for being an idiot who thought he could handle more than he actually could.

He'd always tended to jump and then look to see where he might land. Usually, that worked out for him. But afterward he realized exactly how far he'd jumped and the risks he'd taken, and then the probably-shouldn't-have-done-that crept in.

"What other skills have you been hiding?" Irina asked playfully, unaware of his internal freak-out.

He liked the playful and the way it distracted him from… himself. His body also liked the playful, maybe a little too much. Because while the question wasn't seductive, this was Irina, and he was all kinds of turned on and turned around when they were together lately.

He opened his mouth to say something inappropriate about bedroom skills, but decided against it.

"That's it." He did his best to plaster on his happy-go-lucky face. "I can help in an emergency, and write a killer riff." He'd gone for happy, but it sounded kinda sad, even to him.

"Help?" Irina lifted her eyebrows. "You did more than help. You are a hero."

That killed the dose of turned-on he'd been nursing, and made him itch all over. He was nobody's hero.

Didn't want to be a hero or accept the responsibility that came along with it.

He'd just been in the right place at the right time. Or the wrong place at the wrong time, depending on how a guy looked at it.

"Hey." Irina used her fingertip against his jaw to turn his face to hers. "What's going on?"

He liked the little touch. Maybe it was platonic and perhaps it was the kind of thing she'd have done for anyone. Even him, long before they decided to get married. All the same, dammit, he enjoyed her touch.

"Nothing's going on." He turned back to the window to count the cars they passed.

He hadn't done the car counting thing since he was a kid.

"What is so interesting out there?" Irina peeked around him to glance out the window.

"When I was a kid, I used to count the number of cars that passed when I'd be doing the parent swap on Saturdays."

Back then it was easier to count than to think about what he left behind and what came next. Because he never really fully knew what came next. "It was easier than being angry."

"It's okay to be angry when your parents are going through a divorce," Irina said, moving her hand to his and giving him a squeeze.

He shook his head. "They didn't need that from me. They needed me to be a good kid, so that's what I was."

"That's why you counted cars instead of telling them they made you mad?" she asked.

He didn't answer. Instead he squeezed her hand tighter. He'd been what his parents needed, that's what a guy did when he loved the people in his life.

"What's wrong, Knox?"

This intimacy between them didn't feel so platonic, and what did it say that he didn't mind?

"It could've been bad on the plane." He squeezed harder, grateful to have something to hold onto.

Scratch that, grateful to have Irina to hold onto.

"Baby Jeremy and Cathy are fine." She turned her body a little to face him better. "You jumped right in there. If you hadn't? Craig would've had to deliver their baby in coach with all the people watching." A little smile ticked at the edge of her mouth. "Now it's a story they'll always remember and can tell little Jeremy when he gets older—he was welcomed to the world in first class by a genuine rock star. That baby is destined for great things with a story like that."

"Or maybe she should've been in a hospital or at an airfield in the back of an ambulance," he countered.

"No, the only alternative they had is that Daddy delivered him in coach back near the toilet." She pulled a face. "Doesn't have the same ring as rock star in first class, don't you think?"

She was right, the story was pretty kickass.

Except…

"What if the baby was preterm?" he asked, because the thought had been gnawing at the back of his skull since they'd left the airport and he hit the adrenaline crash.

Irina could've moved her hand away from his.

She didn't.

"What if he was?" she quizzed. "What would you have done?"

They'd covered this in the coursework he'd taken, and he'd regurgitated it for the test. "I would've done my best to stabilize him until we landed. Same with Mom. If things got really bad, we'd have called in for help and had a doctor walk me through."

"And if he didn't breathe right away?" Irina asked, putting a voice to the things he didn't want to think about but that had the potential to eat a hole in his stomach like an ulcer.

He closed his eyes. "I don't want to think about that."

"What would you have done?" Irina pressed, still holding his hand, still allowing herself to be his lifeline.

"Cleared the airway," he said. "Massaged to wake him up. Used the supplemental oxygen, if I needed it, or started helping him breathe manually."

Irina grinned with pride. "See, you knew what to do. That's why you were so awesome. Even if things had gone badly, you would've handled it. Because—" She poked him in the arm. "You are a rock star in more ways than one and you *knew* what to do."

She was right. Maybe the adrenaline was gone, but he'd still done something that helped someone.

He liked this. Enjoyed having her talk to him like this. Enjoyed her hand held in his and the way her earnest eyes tried to convince him what she said was the truth.

"Thank you." He lifted his thumb to her mouth, brushing the pad there at her bottom lip.

He shouldn't have done it. It wasn't even kind of platonic,

and it took things too far. What they had wasn't *that* when they were just *them*. *That* only came when they were putting on a show for everyone else.

Irina sucked in a breath. "Knox, I think we need to—"

"We're at the Performing Arts Complex," the driver announced, pulling into the drop-off zone.

"We need to what?" he asked, even though he didn't want to hear what she would say. Of course, she'd say they needed to cool things off. This wasn't what they'd discussed and didn't make sense when they weren't supposed to be *that*.

Maybe he needed a beer and a nap?

Yeah, that's probably what he needed. He could go home, check out the progress on the paint and the carpet, and enjoy his new refrigerator and the way it cooled the hell out of a Coors.

"Never mind." She released his hand, smoothing her skirt. "Wish me luck?"

"You're the most talented actress I've ever met," he whispered, meaning the words.

The woman could say the name Sergio a thousand different ways, and each way was better than the next.

She had this audition in the bag.

"There are legit big names trying for this role." She shook her head. "At least I got an audition, and there's always that potential for luck."

"You don't need luck," he said. "You're going to go in there, get up on that stage, and break both your legs."

That bought him a grin. "You're pretty awesome, Jeremy Dillion."

"You are, too," he said as her door opened. "Go get 'em, Noodle Cup."

"You're so weird." She winked, grinned, and went off to chase her dreams.

Unfortunately, that left him alone in the back of an SUV headed to a mansion where he'd live by himself, to a life he didn't realize was so empty until Irina slid out of the car and into her own world.

Alone didn't have to suck, though. There were lots of things he could do by himself.

For example, he could call his buddies and make them come hang out with him.

That's what he'd do.

He dropped a call to Linx first, because Linx was the one most likely to not be asleep at one in the afternoon.

This was mostly because he didn't have a newborn keeping him up at odd hours, like Bax, and his wife worked normal hours during the day, so he putzed around until she came back in the late afternoon.

"S'up," Linx said. "You need bailed out of jail?"

Knox snort-laughed. One time. That happened one time. "Nah, I'm back in Denver."

He gave the rundown of Irina's audition, his mom's appearance in Los Angeles, and their quick trip home.

Linx drew an audible breath at the mention of Knox's mom, because he knew how she pushed all of Knox's buttons.

The thing Knox did not mention was that he'd seen a random cervix ten thousand feet in the air, or that he'd had the chance to try the slippery baby hold they talked about in his EMT course. Good news about that, it totally worked.

"I'm feeling the need to hit up Brek's Bar," Linx announced. "Meet there?"

"I was gonna go home first," Knox said.

"Why, because you're like ninety-five and you need to check the mail?" Linx snorted at his own joke even though it wasn't that funny.

"I don't need to check my mail. I just wanted to check the progress and ensure the foreman is getting shit done."

"Do it after a beer?"

Fine. Knox grinned. "See you at Brek's."

"I'll track Bax's ass down and bring him, too," Linx

added. "It'll be the three of us tying one on, just like the old days."

"Except you've got a wife to get to home to by five, and Bax has a wife and a kid to get home to, and I've got to check that the paint dried."

"True story," Linx conceded. "Which means we have about three and a half hours to make it count."

See? Being alone didn't totally suck. If he wasn't alone he couldn't call his bandmates and plan afternoon shenanigans.

That's how he found himself in a booth at Brek's Bar with his original two bandmates, laughing about the time Linx got his ass stuck in one of the equipment storage bins. God, they'd had to grease him up to get him out. The guy had totally been covered by Crisco.

"You miss it?" Linx asked. "The crazy shit we used to do?"

"Nah." Bax shook his head. "We get to watch Tanner and Mach go through it through the lens of experience."

"And I don't have to work on my pick-up game anymore since Becca already agreed to hang out with my ass for life." Linx took a pull from his beer bottle.

Linx didn't drink beer, though. Not anymore. He had the bartender replace the beer with ginger ale so no one would know he preferred life without the buzz of liquor, and he still got to hang onto his rock star card.

"You ever think about what you'd do if you didn't have her?" Knox asked, purely for scientific purposes.

"Why would I do that?" Linx shivered. "Life got good when she showed up."

"What about you?" Knox asked, eyeing Bax. "You ever wish you and Courtney could go back to hating each other?"

Bax shook his head and set his beer—the real thing— back on the table. "Nope. I prefer kissing her to fighting with her. She's a great kisser."

Linx slid him side-eye. "She's my sister. Let's not, yeah?"

Where did that leave Knox? It left him with a marriage to a woman who only saw him as a ticket to where she wanted to be. And where she wanted to be was in a future where he was disposable. He couldn't be pissed about that either, because he'd agreed that she was disposable, too.

Though now he realized there was no way he could continue thinking that about her.

"I think I'm falling for Irina," Knox said, peeling at the label of his beer bottle with the edge of his thumbnail. "Not like we'd talked about with the pretend bullshit, but like I think I might actually really have feelings for her. The don't-want-to-be-with-other-women kind."

Voicing it out loud didn't sound as bad as he thought it might.

"You seriously don't want to be with other women?" Linx asked, lines forming between his brows. "Asking for clarity."

"Right." Knox nodded. "I don't know what that means for me. Not really."

"Because the thought of being with the same person for forever makes you want to peel off your skin with a toothpick?"

Knox may have described his aversion to all things long-term with that analogy at one point.

"That's the thing. When Irina was with me on the plane, I started to wonder if it'd be so bad with her. The whole forever thing would blow, but maybe not *all* the time." Which majorly messed with his head.

"This complicates things," Bax said, even though he didn't need to because it was already clear as all hell.

"She talks way too much, but I enjoy being with her anyway. Her eye color changes every day, but I like the surprise. And she kisses…" He dropped back against the leather of the booth. "God, the woman can kiss."

"Better than a seven-point five?" Linx asked, clearly trying to lighten things up, but Knox was too serious for that.

"Yeah." Knox grinned. "She's a ten. If Becca wanted to give up her title, I'd make her Queen of the Tens."

Tens being the pet name they gave their groupies. Justin had his Beliebers, Lady Gaga had her Little Monsters, and Dimefront had their Tens. Linx's wife, Becca, decreed herself Queen of the Tens after being their numero uno groupie one summer.

"Then I guess the question is"—Bax plunked his bottle on the table—"what are you going to do about it?"

That was the problem.

Knox had no idea if he should even think about it.

Which meant he wasn't going to do *anything* and hope like hell they'd let it alone.

Chapter Twelve
IRINA

THE AUDITION WENT WELL.

Not great, in the sense that they didn't immediately offer a callback or the job. But good in the sense that Irina had totally nailed the Sergio line. Turned out, she just needed a spotlight to make it come alive.

"Hey." She strode through the door to Bax and Courtney's house. Linx, Bax, and Knox all lounged in the living area off the foyer. The television was on in the background, but they were obviously working on a song because Knox and Linx had their guitars out. Linx sat on the couch with his guitar while Knox sat cross-legged on the floor near the dark mahogany coffee table with his.

There were random "heys" given all around. Knox even flashed her a quick grin before going back to his chords.

"Knox, Courtney wants the details of today's excursion from you because I have none of the, and I'm quoting—" She made finger quotes. "Good notes. By good notes, I think she means the messy details. All I could tell her was my hand almost broke, you knew what to do, and the baby's super cute."

Courtney followed her through the door. "Courtney also

wants to understand why you didn't let your publicist know you completed a random, and totally awesome, act of heroism without telling her anything about it."

Irina held up a finger. "Nope. He doesn't like hero word. Don't, uh…go there…"

"I am going to go there because it's true." Courtney wandered through the room to where Bax lounged with Harley mouthing a green horse-shaped baby rattle. She lifted her daughter and blew a raspberry at her tummy. "As your publicist I need to know these things. And as your manager, Hans also needs to know these things so he can handle any damage control or fallout."

"What are you two talking about?" Bax asked, standing to give his wife a welcome-home hug.

Linx grunted something that sounded like, "Yeah, what's going on?"

"You didn't tell them?" Courtney glared at Knox. "It's like you've done something that can totally revive your image and you aren't using it to the full advantage."

"Because it's not for that." Knox blew a breath out from between his lips, and went back to scribbling on the sheet music.

Irina didn't like the way he shut down about it, but she understood emotions got complicated around things some-times. "Maybe we should wait until Becca can come by?"

She understood emotions better than all of them combined.

"Not necessary," Knox said, finally dropping the pen and setting the guitar aside. "Lady had a baby on the plane coming into Denver. Not a big deal."

"Uh." Irina crossed her arms and tapped her foot. "There's more, Knox."

"Why do I feel like there's a lot more?" Bax asked, nuzzling Courtney's neck from behind.

"He delivered the damn baby!" Courtney threw this out almost like an accusation.

"Holy shit," Linx said, dropping the guitar pick he'd held between his lips. "Like you actually put your hands there and…" He made a pulling motion.

"Yup." Irina nodded. "Baby and Mom are both fine because Knox knew what to do. Also, he's a certified EMT—like the guys you call from 9-1-1 that show up with an ambulance. He's even paid the extra five dollars for the certification card." Perhaps she got a little too worked up about that, because she got more and more high pitched toward the end. She cleared her throat and uncrossed her arms. What could she say? She was proud of him.

"How did your audition go?" Knox asked, totally defecting the spotlight back to her.

"Under normal conditions I would be perfectly fine with that question." She crossed her arms. "But you need to let us give you props for the thing you did that was awesome."

She uncrossed her arms, then crossed them again.

Knox didn't say anything, he just stared at her as though waiting for a real answer to his question.

"Audition went fine, they said thanks for coming and they'd be in touch. I've been through this enough to know that usually means they've got someone else lined up they'd prefer to take the role." She dropped to the sofa. "I can't let myself be sad. It's just one audition."

"But you really wanted that part," he said, low and soft.

She flicked a piece of lint from the couch and hedged. "I always want the role. But enough about me, let's talk about you." See? She could deflect right back at him.

"Let's not."

"Knox." Courtney used a tone that Irina knew meant she was all business. "You and I and Hans all have to talk about this."

"Nope." He went right back to strumming his guitar.

"I don't think you're going to get anywhere." Irina's heart softened at the persistent way Knox avoided meeting everyone's gaze.

"She's correct," Knox added, and he looked at her that time. There was something different about the way his gaze caught with hers—comfortable and new all at the same time. "While I have your attention, I'm going to ask that no one tell anyone about this. I'm not doing the hero gig."

Irina had to make a conscious effort not to press him further.

"Let's talk about something else," he suggested.

"Why are you over here?" Irina asked, fidgeting with the edge of a beige throw pillow. "I figured you'd be enjoying your fancy new black bedroom carpet over at your new digs."

"Yeah." Knox gave a little head shake. "Funny story."

Irina stilled. "Why do I think I'm not going to like this story?"

"Because the house is still pink, and even though they deodorized the carpets…again…it still smells a little like piss." He set aside the guitar and stretched. "Which means we've got to figure shit out for the big ceremony."

Yes. Yes they did, because—

"What?" Irina didn't mean for it to sound so dramatic. But there it was, sounding all dramatic. "What happened? They said it'd be done last week." They had, Knox had even confirmed with them and then confirmed with her.

"Painters walked off before they got started. Something about the foreman being a dick. And the carpet was delayed because…the carpet was delayed." He seemed genuinely sorry this happened, so she couldn't even rally a solid dose of upset.

"We're getting married in like five days." Did she point it out for his benefit or hers? She couldn't really say. She ran her fingers through the hair at her temples, holding them there like she was trying to hold her brain together.

"Yeah." He grimaced. "Maybe we should move to Bax's yard? He's got the pirate ship."

Was he being serious? He was being serious.

She'd planned this entire thing and in none of her plans had she included anything pirate-related, because it was a wedding for two adults.

"You have to ask before you get hitched on the pirate ship," Bax said, like this was a given.

"Can we get married on your pirate ship?" Knox asked, not missing a beat.

"Yeah," Bax replied. "But seeing as I'm the captain, I have to perform the ceremony. If you can get an EMT certificate, I can get one of those wedding performer certificates."

"You mean a certificate to be an officiant?" Courtney asked.

Irina wasn't liking at all where this afternoon had gone.

How had they gone from skipping crappy crepes with his mother, to delivering a baby on an airliner, to actively discussing getting hitched on a pirate ship play structure?

Yes, the pirate ship would be sorta fun and kind of different, if they were having a five-year-old's birthday party. Gah, it wasn't like she had a lot to work with.

"Would you be down if we cut out some of the trees before the ceremony, so the helicopter can still do a flyover?" she asked. At least they'd have that.

"Uh," Bax glowered at her. "I like the trees. I like the environment and the way those trees make oxygen for my kid. So, yeah, that *would* be a problem."

Right, no pirate ship for them. They needed a Plan C.

"Shit." Irina rubbed at the center of her forehead. "There's an answer here."

"Maybe you don't let anyone inside the house?" Courtney suggested. "Then the carpet doesn't matter."

"They're gonna need bathrooms," Knox countered.

"Because I don't really want anyone to pee in my bushes, except me."

"We could rent portable restrooms," Courtney suggested, problem-solving on the fly. Which was helpful, since Irina's brain wasn't functioning correctly. Or at all.

Porta-Potties? At her wedding?

"Ew. No." Irina was not okay with that idea. "No. No. I require flush toilets at all my weddings."

"How many do you think you'll have?" Linx asked, and he seemed genuinely interested in the answer.

"Maybe three? Four if it works out?" She'd cap it there, for sure.

Linx blinked hard at her.

"It's not a surprise. I've got a binder for the first three. Number four will probably have to be an elopement because I don't think I've got it in me to do four *big* weddings." Funny that talking about all the weddings wasn't the good time it usually was. "That seems excessive, you know?" she continued. "How many champagne fountains can one girl have?"

"That is the question, isn't it," Linx said, giving Knox a funny look she couldn't quite translate.

Irina grabbed the throw pillow and held it against her chest, resting her chin against it. "You know what? So what if the carpet is gross. Let's just do it. It's fine."

"It's not like it really counts anyway," Courtney added.

"Exactly," Irina said, the word tripping a little funny in her throat.

Knox made a gurgle noise. "I've gotta…" He stood. "… go." Without saying a word, he walked out the door.

"Uh. What just happened?" Courtney asked.

Irina seconded that, because it felt like something big happened.

"That was Knox's pissed sound," Courtney said. "Why's he pissed?"

Irina maybe knew. Did the "not really counting" part sit sideways in his stomach, too?

She pushed away the feeling. No, that wasn't it. She was just feeling elusive things that didn't really exist, to take her mind off the audition that hadn't turned out like she'd hoped. She had a plan and she'd worked hard for the plan. She'd figured perhaps if she got this gig then it might propel her a little more quickly.

"He's been out of sorts since we got off the plane," she said. "This isn't about the wedding." It wasn't like he didn't know it wasn't a real marriage in the sense of sex, and maybe babies, and forever. "Though it could be about the carpet."

"What's his deal with the plane?" Linx asked, in that Linx way of his where he went from taking nothing seriously to everything.

"I think he's still processing what happened." Irina pulled at a thread of her blouse, snapping it off. "Things were fine, sure, but that wasn't a given and he grabbed on to that responsibility of taking charge without really thinking what could've happened. He's been processing that. Dealing with it all."

"I'll go see what he's up to." Bax pressed a kiss to Courtney's temple, then one to Harley's cheek. "C'mon, Linx. Let them figure out the wedding, we'll sort out the groom."

"Thanks, guys." Irina clasped her hands around the pillow.

"You are welcome to use our house for whatever you need," Bax said before closing the door. "As long as you don't cut down any trees." The last part he hollered through the door.

Irina pulled her feet up under herself. "Let me think for a minute about alternatives."

Though she'd already been through every Denver venue as an option, she hadn't thought about other cities. They could go up to the mountains. Though Knox wouldn't like that because of the bugs.

Maybe they could fly everyone to a beach? He'd love that.

Though that seemed excessive when she'd already put a deposit on the Denver caterer.

"Irina?" Courtney said. "Is Knox okay?"

"I don't know." She didn't, not really. "I don't know what's going on with him."

That wasn't entirely the truth, but it sounded about right.

"The best thing we can do is sort out the wedding details," Irina continued, so she didn't have to think about how well she knew or didn't know Knox. "So he doesn't have to worry about anything other than carpet and paint."

"I have an idea." Courtney continued bouncing little Harley, the wheels clearly turning in her noggin. "What if you *did* do it on the pirate ship? Or even *by* the pirate ship? What do you have to lose?"

"We lose the helicopters," Irina countered. "That's what we lose."

Courtney chewed on that. "If we cancel the real minister, Bax can get ordained online so he won't be grumpy," Courtney continued her thoughts. "And then he can do the ceremony." She grinned. "We may not need the paparazzi helicopters if we get you the cover of *People* magazine. Something like this is actually a really good story." She lifted her eyebrows. "This could work."

"Isn't it a little more eight-year-old birthday party and a whole lot less rock star wedding?" Irina might just have to accept portable restrooms as part of the background of the big day if the alternative was a kid's pirate ship wedding.

"That's the best thing about rock stars, you never know what they're gonna do." Courtney's eyes glinted with what Irina hoped was not misplaced mischief. "We'll go nuts with the twinkle lights for the reception. Still put up the tent for the guests. And we have a florist go bananas with flowers, this time they'll just do it around the ship instead of Knox's yard."

"No paper pirate hats?" Irina confirmed.

"I cannot promise that Bax won't start talking like a pirate during the ceremony." Courtney did the baby bounce thing that calmed Harley right down. "But I can hide all of the paper hats."

"What do I have to lose?"

"Right?" Courtney grinned. "If it ends up sucky, just tack on a fourth wedding."

Irina laughed, but she didn't quite feel the humor all the way in her soul.

Chapter Thirteen

KNOX

MEET-THE-PARENTS AFTERNOON PAR-TAY at Bax and Courtney's digs started any second. Once the bride showed up, things would get serious.

Irina apparently took her party planning to the next level, because over the past days she'd found every excuse she could to add mini events to the big event.

"How'd carpet demo go?" Linx asked.

Knox made a gagging sound.

"That good, huh?" Linx pulled a face.

"Ripping out urine-scented carpet is about as much fun as it sounds," Knox said. Folding his hands behind his head.

He'd viewed a few MyTube videos and figured it wasn't that hard. Ten minutes in, he decided to let the professionals handle the demo. They had to have a better system than he'd come up with. His system being pull, then gag, then pull, then gag some more.

"Carpet isn't going anywhere until the crew comes in," he confirmed. Since the carpet wasn't going anywhere for a while, he'd taken over his old room at Bax's place. It worked because with all the family coming in, there was food everywhere. Good food. Lots of cookies, too.

No pie, but he held out hope that Irina would come through on that.

Staying here worked out, since Irina decided they should get married on the pirate ship in the backyard after all.

As a man who was once a third grader, he was automatically agreeable to getting married on playground equipment. Especially the kind where he could talk with a pirate accent, and no one would think he'd lost his marbles.

Besides, Courtney had all kinds of publicist-type ideas of how they could get him not-an-asshole articles taking the pirate ship angle.

Bowl of tortilla chips in one hand, and two smaller bowls of guac in the other, Linx dropped on the couch beside Knox. Right up in his space. Also holding no regard for personal space, Bax took the other side, holding a plate of little cucumber sandwiches.

They both wore black jeans and a T-shirt with a fancy suit screen-printed on the front. The only difference between their outfits and Knox's was that the back of his had the word *Groom*.

Bax's read *Minister*. And then in tiny words underneath Courtney had added, *I paid $5 for the certificate card.*

What the hell, Knox laughed at it. Certificate cards came in handy and were absolutely worth the extra few bucks.

Linx's read *Ring Bearer*, since he'd walk Harley—their flower girl—down the aisle. Seeing as she was a baby and didn't even crawl yet, she needed a lift.

Tanner and Mach were their groomsmen.

"Are you actually eating those things?" Knox eyed the tea sandwich platter because he seriously doubted whether those actually qualified as sandwiches. They'd been cut into sunflowers, which seemed an affront to all sandwiches everywhere.

"Try one." Bax held it up.

Ew.

"I'm not eating that. It's a water-vegetable, cheese mix on white bread." No, thank you. "Who even approved cucumber sandwiches?"

"Tanner's friends over at the retirement home catered today. You should've had them do the wedding, too." Bax popped one in his mouth. "They soak the cucumbers in vodka overnight, then they add extra vodka to the cream cheese mix. I'm not sure, but I think they even bake it in the bread." Bax popped another one. "I've never been drunk on sandwiches before, but I figured I'll give it a try while I have the chance. For science."

What the fuck, Knox had tried weirder. He snagged a tiny little sandwich and licked at the cream cheese along the edge. The damn thing tasted like a distillery. He tossed it down his throat and grabbed another.

"What do they put in the guac?" He leaned over to Linx's chip bowl.

"Spicy." Linx held up one bowl. "Not spicy." He gestured to the other.

Knox scooped some spicy.

Tequila.

"Not spicy is the ring-bearer version." Linx kicked back, enjoying his apparently virgin guac.

"I'd suggest not mixing your booze," Bax suggested to Knox, entirely too seriously for a guy getting drunk on cucumber tea sandwiches. "Stick with one or the other."

Knox turned toward the table of food that looked surprisingly normal, but apparently had been spiked with all the liquor in the Cherry Creek area. This would make the parental meet and greet substantially more tolerable.

"Table's too far." He popped another sandwich.

One wouldn't think vodka and cucumber tea sandwiches would actually taste good, but the amount of vodka made him not even care that he was eating a vegetable.

Fuck, if they'd added vodka to his vegetables in high school, maybe he'd actually have eaten them more often.

"Which of your parents called first-round pick?" Bax asked around another shot of sandwich.

The guys had all grown up on the same street back in the day. Bax and Linx's parents stayed together, so that left Knox as the odd man out when the divorce was final. Bax's garage had been his lifeline during those years.

That's when they'd come up with the idea to start a band, and Dimefront was born.

"Dad got here before her, so he called dibs." Knox scarfed another sammie. A handful of these and he wouldn't care that his parents were a mess, the woman he was marrying had already planned a divorce, and his house was a combination of pink and piss.

Dad bunked at Linx's place. Mom stayed at the Marriott near the airport because being across the street from his dad was entirely too close. Dad called dibs on the first hour of the get-together. Mom agreed to come after. It took some convincing, but Dad conceded to leaving before her car drove up. She agreed to notify them when she was ten minutes out.

Honestly, it'd been the best communication they'd had as a family in over twenty years.

"The whole thing is stupid, and they should learn to be in the same room together," Knox said, expressly not grabbing another sandwich because he should probably try to stand up when Irina's parents arrived.

"You come up with a plan yet to show Irina she can't live without you?" Linx asked, still munching on chips.

"My plan is to marry her." Knox frowned, because that's as far as he'd gotten with the plan. Which meant it was more of a one-item to-do list versus an actual laid-out plan.

"All right." Linx set the chips and guac on the coffee table, and brushed the salt from his hands onto his jeans. "Here's what we're gonna do. First thing? We're coming up with a plan."

"Becca loves when I sing to her. You tried that?" Linx asked, scooping more guacamole.

"No." Knox elbowed them both, so they'd give him some space.

Linx clapped his hands like he'd done something special. "Then that's step one."

"Step two is to cook for her," Bax nodded as he spoke. "That worked for Courtney."

"I already cooked for her."

"It didn't work?" Bax asked.

Knox shook his head. "Clearly."

"Maybe it's what you cooked for her," Linx added.

"Then what should I cook for her?"

Bax shrugged. "It's not really about the food. Have her sit on the countertop while you're heating shit up and then see if she'll let you go down on her while it's in the oven."

"That is the stupidest idea I've ever heard."

"And yet here you are marrying a chick with her foot out the door while we sit here married to chicks who are entirely out of our league." Bax shrugged. "But what the fuck do we know?"

"The key is that you've got to show her how great it could be with you," Linx said. "She's not gonna see that all on her own. You need to nudge it along."

Knox had always figured relationships were hard, always figured they weren't worth the time. But watching Bax and Courtney, Linx and Becca, and the way he'd developed a case of feelings toward his future wife…well, he'd realized that relationships didn't have to suck. Not like his parents had.

Hell, if he could convince himself to give it a shot, getting Irina on board would be a cakewalk.

That's when the door blew open—figuratively—and Irina

waltzed in with her parents. He'd met her mom, but not her dad.

Irina had gone with a flowing yellow gown and pinned a matching flower in her now blonde hair. Sunshine and summertime was the vibe she exuded. He enjoyed both of those things, so he was all into the mood she brought with her.

Knox stood, glad he'd only had two vodka sandwiches since they hit him like a truck.

"You don't have to say a word." The man with Irina walked across the room straight to Bax. Bax, who still sat on the couch.

"I'm Sparrow," Irina's dad's eyes danced just like his daughter's. "It's nice to finally meet my future son-in-law." He held out his hand to Bax.

Bax finished chewing his latest sandwich and shook the man's hand. "Nice to meet—"

"Dad." Irina hurried to them. "That's not Knox." Irina looped her arm with his. "*This* is Knox."

Irina pulled him against her side.

"You met my mom, Janis." Irina started the introductions. "This is my dad, Eugene. Bu-u-ut everyone calls him Sparrow."

They'd been engaged for a decent number of days, known each other even longer, and honest as all hell he did not know they called her dad Sparrow.

"Nice to meet you… Sparrow." He didn't mean to pause, or internally seize at the thought of birds, it just happened. "And Janis, always a pleasure."

Janis seemed to be a future version of Irina with a similar flower in her hair, though she wore what he could only describe as an orange floral-printed flowing jumpsuit. Her flower was orange.

Sparrow wore a pastel-blue seventies-style suit. The vintage style that'd made a comeback recently, so it didn't look out of place. Mostly, it seemed trendy. If Knox were into that stuff, which he wasn't. Not until all the wedding planning made him start paying attention to shit.

Knox dropped a kiss to the top of Irina's head, because he could.

"Sorry about that, son," Sparrow held his hand to Knox. "I'd know you anywhere."

"Dad, stop," Irina said, between her teeth.

"You have no idea how happy we are that Irina found a nice musician for her first husband," Irina's dad said as her mom looped an arm with Knox's other side.

"We worried she'd end up with an accountant or some nonsense like that," her mom added.

"That's not me." Knox wasn't entirely sure what to do with himself since the two women had sandwiched him in between them. "I do have an accountant though."

"We won't hold that against you," Sparrow put his hands on his hips.

They finished the introductions to the rest of the band members and Hans, Becca, and Courtney. Though it was Harley who stole the show.

This was not a surprise given that she was the cutest of all of them.

His dad ambled over, and it was only slightly weird, since he was an accountant and Sparrow regurgitated the accountant joke for him.

"This is going so well," Irina whispered once everyone was good and drunk off the appetizers.

"That's because my mom hasn't shown up yet," he whispered back.

"I gave them a heads-up about your mom." Irina grimaced. "Hope that's okay."

"There's no way to get the full heads-up on my mother, but it was nice of you to give it a try."

Irina gave him a soft smile. A smile he realized she didn't

use very often, but when she did it made him feel twenty feet tall. "You doing okay with all the family stuff?"

"I get to marry a pretty girl on a pirate ship in a couple of days." He stuffed his hands in his pockets because what he really wanted to do was reach out and touch the flower in her hair. While he could do that, and it wouldn't be out of place for a future groom to touch the flower hair of his future bride, he needed to rein it in.

"It's like I get to live out my preteen fantasy as a grown-up," he said instead of touching her.

That's when things went a little sideways, because the doorbell rang.

The doorbell rang but everyone was already there.

He glanced around and his extremities all turned numb when his gaze landed on Dad chatting it up with Bax's parents near the kitchen.

Everyone was present…except his mother.

Chapter Fourteen

IRINA

"I DON'T UNDERSTAND why his father has to leave so his mother can arrive?" Mom seemed genuinely conflicted at the hostility rattling around Knox's family.

Honestly, so was Irina. There was lots about Knox she didn't understand. As the days went by, she wanted more and more to unravel that tangle.

His dad decided *not* to leave, negotiations fell apart, and now his parents both pretended to ignore each other from opposite sides of the room, while also giving one another massively dirty looks. Not the fun kind that meant they'd be happy later, either. Full on murderous.

"Is this like that superhero movie where the billionaire couldn't be in the same room with the bat guy because they were the same person?" Dad asked.

"No, Dad. It's nothing like that because they are actually different people." Different people who actively disliked one another.

"But Knox is so lovely." Mom eyed Knox, who had let his mother in the door and then started sweating from his earlobes. "How did such argumentative people end up with such a lovely son?"

Honestly, Irina had no idea. None at all.

Knox shuffled his mom in their direction. She had the expression like she'd eaten an entire bag of sour gummies.

Irina could relate and for real considered going to hang out with the pink urine carpet instead of her own party.

Knox got closer and Irina channeled a confident character she'd once played at community theater who spent her summers as a spy. The badass character came in handy sometimes.

"Mom," Irina said, hoping to heavens she'd behave and not go off about family hostilities and how that affected the butterflies of the Southern Hemisphere. "You remember Beverly, Knox's mother," Irina continued.

"Beatrice," Knox murmured.

Irina froze.

Shit. Shit. Shit.

"Right. It's Beatrice." Irina mouthed "help me" to him, but at this point even his ability to be cute probably wouldn't save her.

"You know, we had a goat once named Beatrice." Mom was all grins. "I loved her. We used to milk her every morning before we sold her to the neighbor guy because he decided to start making soap. That's when I took up painting."

Funny, to Irina that all made perfect sense. To everyone else? Probably not.

Irina did wish her mom hadn't mentioned the milking, but at least she didn't go on about her theory of world anger wrecking butterfly ecosystems.

Knox's mom frowned. "I don't know what that has to do with anything."

"Goat milk soap?" Mom made a rubbing motion on the back of her hands. "It's wonderful. Beatrice's milk made great soap. Have you ever made soap?"

"No." Beatrice gave Knox the same kind of look Irina had just given him. The "help me" one.

"Well, you haven't lived until you've had real goat milk soap." Mom smiled, but it seemed a bit forced.

"There's food?" Beatrice—why couldn't she say her freaking name correctly?—eyed the table of drunken appetizers.

"Yeah." Knox had shoved his hands in his pockets again. He did that a lot lately. "You should help yourself. Eat up. Eat lots."

Beatrice—see, she could remember it when she didn't have to say it—headed for the food table.

"Knox?" Courtney hurried through the guests. "Did you do this?" She held up her phone.

There on one of the biggest tabloid sites was a picture of Knox on the plane holding the baby. The headline made it clear he handled the delivery. As in, full-on handled it. With his hands.

Knox took the phone, flipping through the images.

"These are the photos you took," Knox said to Irina, seemingly unbelieving.

Wasn't that just a vote of confidence?

He looked to Courtney. "Did you send these?"

His tone was full icicle and not the kind with booze mixed in for fun.

She didn't appreciate that tone. Holding up her hands, she shook her head. "You know I think it's great for your image, but you told me to leave it alone. I did."

He glanced to Irina. "Was it you?"

Seriously? She resented the question.

"I didn't sell you out, if that's what you're asking." She crossed her arms because she didn't like the feeling of being exposed. Or the feeling that came with Knox's sort-of accusation.

"I get it." He handed the phone back to Courtney.

"What do you get?" Irina asked.

"I get that you wanted me to be the hero. Congratulations, I'm the hero. The photos are out, now we don't have to do this." His lips thinned as he spoke.

Hers probably did too, right along with her blood, and the little space between her eyebrows.

"This?" she asked, since he should probably clarify

"The wedding." He stuck his hands on his hips.

"You think I don't want to do the wedding?" she asked, because everything she'd done over the past months had been to *do* the wedding.

"This is just like your mom and I's wedding," Knox's dad said from the doorway to the kitchen, cheerful as though this was a good thing. "Right, Beatrice?"

Beatrice crossed her arms in a close imitation of Irina's. "No, she hasn't started to cry because she realized she's supposed to spend her entire life with the world's greatest putz."

Without even the slightest hesitation, Knox's dad hopped right into the ring. "You know, if you'd been nicer—"

"What if—" Courtney snapped both fingers. "We moved this conversation, so it's not happening in front of all the parentals?"

"Yeah." Irina huffed through the hurt, then strode to the hallway that led to the wing of the house with their bedrooms. She went to her bedroom instead of his, for no other reason than home-field advantage seemed like a good idea.

She didn't need to look to see if Knox followed her, she could tell he did by the thud of his gait behind her.

He closed the door behind him. "Irina."

Oh boy, he said a whole lot with just her name.

"I have a quick question." She held up a hand like she was in school. "What have I done to make you think I don't want to get married? Was it the planning of the ceremony? Or the effort I put into the reception?"

"I'm just saying it makes sense to leak the photos if you

don't want to see this through," he said, as though she hadn't gotten that from the before conversation.

"Why aren't you grilling Courtney?" she asked. "Or, I don't know, Grace. Or Cathy or Craig? Hans? Where the hell is Hans, and how do you know he didn't do it?" She went back to her resting actress pose with arms crossed in front of her. "Because I took the photos, yes. But I took them on Craig's phone. You posed for them, so you know I took 'em. Maybe—" She held up her little-bit fingers. "You should take it down a notch, Mr. Taking-Things-Too-Far."

They stared at each other for one beat, two, then three.

Knox's pissed-off facade cracked. "Fuck." He smiled a timid smile. "I'm an asshole."

"Well, we're trying to fix that. Aren't we?" she countered.

"Fuck." Knox dropped to sit at the end of her bed.

She didn't love that, because mostly right now she wanted to strangle him for implying she'd expose him after he'd asked her not to.

"What's going on with this whole thing, anyway?" she asked. "It's not like someone dropped a sex tape. I don't get the unwillingness to be a hero."

"I don't know," he said. But he said it in that way people said things when they actually did know, but they didn't want to admit that they knew.

"And, also," she went on. "We are getting married because Courtney has an entire spread prepared for *People* magazine that involves you, me, and a pirate ship. I like the way my life is going since you agreed to marry me and we started this whole thing."

"You like the way your life is going?" he asked, out-of-place confusion on his face.

"Yes, I do." She sat beside him, not touching because she still sort of worried what might happen if they touched each other again in private. "Do you?"

"I don't hate it," he admitted. "I wanted to hate this whole thing a lot more."

"This whole thing being me?" The question was light and not heavy. They didn't need to do heavy. This thing between them didn't need to have weight. It wasn't a winter-parka type of relationship. More like a light jacket.

"The wedding," he said. "I don't hate hanging out with you. Or the rest of it."

The relationship? She wanted to ask, to use the word, but if he had a problem with the hero word, he'd probably not appreciate the relationship word.

"Look, Knox." She nudged him with the edge of her thigh. "The hanging out with you and all the other stuff is pretty awesome. So, let's just continue not hating it and let it do what we need it to do. But I'm straight with you, next time you want to accuse me of something before you have any evidence to the contrary, please don't. It hurts my feelings."

"Thank you for not leaking those photos." He dropped his head to his hands. "Hans didn't do it. I know that. Craig and Cathy knew I didn't want them out, so they probably wouldn't. They said they owed me and that's the favor I asked. Grace…yeah? Could've been Grace?"

It didn't really matter since they were well and truly leaked. "They're out there. Just let it be what it can be for you."

He shook his head. "No comment is my only comment to the press about them."

"Because you don't want to be a hero?" This was really his hill to die on. "There are so many worse things."

He kept his face in his hands as he said, "Because heroes are relied on. I'm not that guy. Not the person people count on."

"I don't know that that's the truth." She'd sort of started to enjoy depending on him.

Irina's phone chimed in her purse. The special ringtone she used for casting directors and her agent.

She pulled it out, hopeful that maybe someone had an actress emergency and needed her presence immediately, so she wouldn't have to walk back out and try to save face in front of everyone.

The message was from the casting director for the play.

"Oh my God." Irina blinked at the message. "Holy crap."

They want me. Well, maybe they want me. They don't not want me.

"Good news?" Knox asked, pulling himself from his funk.

"Uh…" Irina did a little shimmy number. "I got a callback. The callback. Holy crap." She wiped at her forehead like she was taking her temperature.

The shot of adrenaline helped wipe out any residual grumpy with Knox and his implication she might be a big leaking jerkface. "It's happening, Knox."

"You deserve it." He stood. "We should celebrate."

"Yes. Celebrate." Irina squeed.

"Good thing we've got a champagne fountain on tap for tomorrow," he said. "Is the big callback after the honeymoon or do we need to postpone the islands?"

Well, she hadn't read that far. Instead of answering, Irina scrolled through the instructions, her heart dropping a little with each line and the scrolling slowing with each word.

"What? Are they requiring a blood sacrifice?" he joked.

Actually, that might be easier than the real issue. She took a deep breath. There was always a solution when things looked like they wouldn't work out.

Phone still in her palm, she glanced up to her groom.

Yes, there was always a solution.

"No, things are fabulous," she said. "I got a callback." She sang that last part singsong.

They were. Everything was fine.

Even if the callback she'd waited her whole life for was scheduled during her wedding.

Chapter Fifteen
KNOX

"IT IS SERIOUSLY HARD to start Operation Make Irina Permanent if she isn't even here," Linx grumbled. The guy was acting like an actual ring bearer—he needed juice, a nap, and someone to comb his hair for him.

"The permanent thing is still up in the air." Knox pulled his bow tie taut.

"Because she's not actually here?" Bax asked.

Well, that didn't help things. But, also, "Because…we haven't renegotiated."

"But you still want to," Bax said, tossing his rolled-up black socks into the air, catching them, then tossing again.

Knox hoped those hadn't been on his feet yet.

"I need time to figure out what I want." Knox sighed.

"How does it make you feel when you think about the divorce?" Linx asked.

"Like you've been married for entirely too long, since you're asking questions like that." Knox shook out his shoulders and grabbed the tuxedo jacket.

"That's not an answer." Linx pursed his lips.

"Fine. I don't want to think about it being over, it makes me edgy," Knox admitted. The thought made him want to eat a box of cookies and listen to Celine Dion songs on repeat. "But thinking about it lasting forever also makes me edgy. Who'd want that? The constant pressure of the same person for every day? I mean, go you two for taking that route. I just happen to like life more than letting one person run my life for the rest of it."

"I don't accept this," Linx said.

"Okay." Knox didn't really care if he accepted it or not. It's how things were.

"So now we've got to add Operation Pull Knox's Head Out of His Ass to our mission?" Bax asked Linx, tossing the socks again.

Knox shrugged on the jacket, smoothing the lapel. "Yeah, good luck with that, boys."

"Still no bride?" Mom asked, sauntering in the room. Really, he wouldn't have put it past his mother to have slashed her tires.

Actually… "You didn't do anything to my bride, did you?"

Because that would be low, but not totally out of the ordinary for the things he'd seen his parents do to each other when ticked off. Once, when Dad complained about the salt level of the chuck roast, Mom poured an entire can of tomato soup in his gas tank.

That hadn't gone over well with Dad or the mechanic.

"What could I have done to her?" Mom asked, faux appalled.

Well, he could start a Game of Thrones style list, but that would probably only serve to freak him the fuck out.

"Seriously, Jeremy." Mom tsked. "Believe it or not, while I want you to be happy, and I think this wedding is a *horrible* idea, I do have some boundaries when it comes to keeping my nose to myself."

Linx snort laughed at that.

"If she's not here," Mom looked around the room like

Irina might pop out from under the bed. "Your people should start with damage control." Mom lifted her hands in mock surrender. Mock, because there was no way she'd ever actually surrender. At least she hadn't dressed all in black for the event like it was a funeral—she'd gone with yellow. "That's all I'm saying."

That's not all she was saying, and they both knew it.

He paced the floor of his room at Bax's place back to the dresser to grab his own pair of socks. The guest room was large, with a king-sized bed, dresser, and all the other shit a bedroom needed. He even had his own en suite bathroom. He appreciated that. The place wasn't his, but it was comfortable enough. Yeah, the mattress could've used an upgrade, and the thread count of the sheets was weak, but it didn't totally suck. Hell, it was better than his official residence because it smelled decent, and the walls didn't look like someone sprayed them down with Pepto.

"You still have time to back out of this," Mom continued, like she hadn't just said that.

"Not happening," he murmured, closing the dresser drawer.

The guests were arriving—or had arrived. Bax and Linx hung with him because they didn't want to deal with people. Mach and Tanner both played interference with guests since they were the newbies, and also because his bride was totally missing in action, and they needed the guests entertained until she arrived.

Was he worried about his bride-to-be? No, because Courtney and Becca were missing right along with her. Missing in the sense they weren't here at the wedding, but not missing because they'd both checked in with their spousal units even though they didn't say where they were. There had been a vague acknowledgement Irina was with them.

"Jeremy, you know I only have your best interests at heart

here," Mom went on, like he'd actually been listening to whatever she'd been going on about.

Knox slipped on his wingtips, seeing as they were supposed to say their vows in…oh…twenty minutes or so. "Mom, seriously, drop it."

"She's not here," Mom did not drop it. "You don't even know that she's coming."

"I do know she's coming. I talked to her this morning." Not long and not about anything as important as, say, not showing up at the wedding, but they'd conversed.

"A lot of things can change in a short time." Mom at least had the decency to look sad while she said this. Big frown, eyelid droop, all of it. She was probably as good an actress as Irina.

That thought dropped on his chest like a weighted blanket.

Irina was an excellent actress.

So was his mother.

Irina was a chameleon.

So was his mother.

He shook his head. That line of thought would do nothing but make him question decisions he'd already made.

Besides, his mother and Irina were nothing alike. Irina used her powers of persuasion for entertainment and good. His mother? Well, she did do good work as a prosecutor, putting the bad guys behind bars. But she wasn't Irina. Didn't have that streak of kindness he'd seen in his future ex-wife.

A quick tap-a-tap on the bedroom door and Tanner joined the Mommy and Me party.

"Hey," Tanner said, eyeing Knox's mom sort of funny.

Mach followed him, doing the same thing. He gave two thumbs up. "Good news, we found your bride."

"Where is she?" Knox wished he had a tray of those cucumber sandwiches with him.

"We have good reason to believe she is running late."

Mach leaned against the wall, like they were discussing what they'd order for dinner. Not where Knox's future ex-wife was when she was supposed to meet him on top of a pirate ship.

"Because she told us she's running late. But she's with Courtney and Becca," Tanner said. "They're *all* running late."

"Literally, running." Mach nodded and made a motion with his index and middle finger like a bride scurrying through the air.

"What the hell was she doing that was more important than this?" Knox asked, sort of hoping it involved baking pie.

"No idea, the answers to those questions were not included when we talked," Tanner said.

Mach snorted. "Talked."

"We talked," Tanner gave his buddy a what-the-fuck look if Knox had ever seen one.

"You asked where she'd been and Becca said to mind your own business," Mach gave the play-by-play.

"Exactly." Tanner fell back on the bed with no care at all that he'd probably wrinkle his tuxedo coat or mess up Knox's carefully made bed. "She said she'll see you at the wedding."

Things moved pretty quickly after that, and he took his time heading to the pirate ship. He figured he'd be more nervous, but oddly his blood pressure didn't seem high, he wasn't sweating abnormally, and he felt like he'd eaten a whole bowl of retirement-home guacamole, because this wedding felt right.

"I'm here." Irina hurried down the hallway, Becca beside her, somehow adding lip gloss to Irina's lips while Irina still hustled.

Knox stilled because she was stunning.

"We're all here," Courtney said, holding a veil in her hand and arranging the tulle.

The bustle of activity that coincided with Irina's arrival all faded into the periphery when their eyes met.

She wasn't wearing the dress she'd clipped and added to her vision mural.

No, she wore the red gown he'd said he wanted.

He did a full tip-to-toe perusal of the gown. He probably looked like an internet meme with the amount of blinking that went on right then for him.

Irina went with blonde hair today and green eyes. He dug it.

She pinned her hair up at the crown of her head, and she looked like a princess—if princesses wore red poufy dresses that showed off a helluva lot of cleavage and had a substantial train behind them. Becca finished with the gloss and moved to arrange the train.

Something about the way Irina looked made him not care the ceremony would start late, or that he'd been sort of worried about where she might've been. Fine, he hadn't been *worried*, worried. Just a little concerned that maybe she'd decided to go eat pie without him.

"You bought my dress." He strode to her, not able to stop the grin spreading across his face.

"Well, *you* bought *my* dress." She pulled at the sides of the skirt. "But I figured since it's the one you wanted, I should listen."

"Look at us, making this marriage work." Wow, shouldn't he be panicking at this point? They were nearly at the altar, his bride looked fan-fucking-tastic, and he was going to pledge his troth for at least the next few months to her. Yet, he remained totally calm.

He reached forward and brushed his fingers at her neckline, which was silly because it was just the two of them. There was no show. Honest as hell, he wasn't trying to look at her cleavage, but she totally had it on display, and it was *right there.*

She smiled at the graze of his fingertips, visible goosebumps forming along her skin. She was a curated jewel he wanted to touch. Just because it didn't make sense to touch her, didn't mean he wouldn't. If anything, he'd never been good at doing what he should.

"You look really pretty, Noodle Cup." He gave the lamest compliment in the history of compliments, but he meant it from the bottom of his soul. She was the prettiest girl he'd ever seen. The fact that they were about to go get hitched on a pirate ship was only the icing on the proverbial cake.

She snorted, lifted herself up on her toes, and pressed a quick kiss to his mouth.

Now, that? That was unexpected.

"You look handsome, too, Knox," she said against his lips before lowering herself to straighten his bow tie.

"Did you want to tell me why we're starting late?" he asked, toying with one of the curls along her neckline.

"Not really." She shook her head, but she grinned while she did it, so he wasn't super worried she'd been exercising her rights to non-disclosure nookie.

Not that it was his concern if she was, he just sort of hoped she wasn't.

Fine, he seriously hoped she wasn't. The thought of it made an imaginary toothpick lodge sideways in his throat.

"You gonna tell me anyway?" he asked.

"The callback was today." She said this like she was confessing something super important. "I got them to move it earlier, but then they wanted me to run other scenes. It took longer…"

"You should've told me." He frowned, and he didn't like frowning when he looked so hot, and she looked so pretty. Those were reasons to smile.

"I didn't want you to feel like this didn't matter." Her breaths came quickly.

"Aren't we supposed to be a team?" he asked. "At least during this whole thing."

She pulled the side of her bottom lip in. "Yes?"

"I'm going to use one of my compromises," he announced. Though he'd sort of hoped he could use them for food-related stuff, this mattered more. "When something is important to us, we tell the other so they can support us."

"Okay," she agreed, quietly.

"Did you get the job?" He lifted his eyebrows, hoping like hell she did.

She nodded and her whole body radiated happiness. "I did."

He liked that happiness for her.

"Wanna get married now?" he asked, waggling his eyebrows like he'd been practicing it in the mirror that morning.

She didn't answer, but she grinned. "You?"

"Eh." He lifted a corner of his lip, and lied. "Not really."

"So let's do it anyway?" she asked, taking his arm with hers.

"Yup," he agreed. "I hear there's a champagne fountain waiting for us at the end."

She laughed, and he led her toward their temporary future.

"Congratulations, Irina," he whispered, and he meant it.

Chapter Sixteen

IRINA

THERE WAS a decent slog across the lawn to get to the playground with the pirate ship, so they'd set up a staging tent that would eventually turn into a reception area.

The sun shone bright in the late afternoon, but not so hot that guests would be uncomfortable. Which was good, since she'd kept them waiting.

She didn't mean to, didn't want to, but what was she supposed to do when the only time they could move her to was within an hour of her first wedding ceremony?

So she'd enlisted her girls and they'd gone on an adventure.

The audition went long so Becca had to help her get into the gown in the back of Courtney's car. That went fine until she accidentally flashed a guy on a motorcycle beside them. She seriously hoped that wouldn't end up on TMZ.

Becca and Courtney helped ensure she made it back with moments to spare. Only a few, but enough so it worked.

That was all then, now was now. She was right where she should be, awaiting her entrance to the ceremony.

The set she'd created on the fly was perfection.

The pirate ship all decked out in red roses that matched

her dress and her bouquet. The florist had no problem pivoting from decorating the arches she'd planned originally to the playground pirate ship they'd ended up with.

By the time his team finished with the flowers, it looked like a fairy tale—roses everywhere, some kind of red flowers draped from anything high enough for them to dangle. The people she loved all waiting for her in satin-covered plastic chairs—her parents, her aunts and uncles. Courtney and all of Dimefront.

The curtain pulled back so Linx and Harley could do the flower girl, ring bearer gig. Then Becca waltzed down the aisle like a badass in creamy white Vera Wang.

With the costuming decision to switch up her wardrobe, Irina had decided that since she'd wear red, the bridesmaids would wear white. It'd been a whole thing that took an entire afternoon to figure out.

Though, at the moment, no one was looking at the white dress Becca wore because—

"What the hell is Bax wearing?" Irina hissed to Courtney. "He promised no pirate hats."

Shit, he'd totally wrecked the ambiance of classy wedding she'd been going for, irreparably pivoting the whole shebang into kid-birthday-party territory.

"Technically, he promised no *paper* pirate hats. I didn't count on him buying the real deal," Courtney said, obviously unamused.

Not just a pirate hat. Bax wore a whole pirate get-up with an actual parrot on his shoulder. A live parrot that likely knew how to talk.

"If that parrot poops on him during your ceremony, I'm going to lose my mind," Courtney said. Mostly, Irina would probably laugh, but still...

"Where did he get the bird?" Irina asked.

Courtney pursed her lips. "God, I hope it's rented and not ours."

"I did not expect this," Irina said, her voice pitching a little wonky.

She cleared her throat.

Courtney shrugged a bare shoulder. "I'll punish him later, I promise."

"Why do I think that won't be a hardship for either of you?" Irina did not love that the people getting laid on her wedding day would be everyone but her.

"Hold up two more seconds and then we're going to have—"

A paparazzo burst through the back of the tent, snapping photos erratically.

Two beefy guys in security uniforms were four steps behind him.

"You planned this?" Irina asked without moving her lips and working on an appalled yet still happy facade.

"Uh-huh." Courtney made a gesture to security, and they closed the gap, removing the photographer from the tent. "Since we don't have helicopters. There's also a guy hiding in one of Bax's favorite trees." She leaned closer and whispered, "He doesn't know."

Oh. Courtney really was on this.

No time to think about that, though, because music played for Courtney's entrance, and she made her way down the aisle.

Irina waited her turn to strut toward Knox like a badass rocker wife. When the bridal march started, she erased herself and slapped on her bridal character for the day.

One foot in front of the other.

She stepped outside and paused. Not because of the pirate who would be marrying her.

Or because she was drinking in the phenomenal job she'd done with their wedding—seriously, it looked great.

No, she paused because this was real.

This wasn't a character.

She was herself.

Knox was smiling at her, his eyes broadcasting that he knew this wasn't a character and clearly he liked that.

How the hell was she supposed to be herself? She'd planned on being the *character*. She loved being the center of attention. Adored when she could play a part and entertain. Funny, though, at the moment, even though she was in full costume, knew her lines like the little freckle on Knox's earlobe…she still felt more exposed than she'd ever felt before.

Get it together, girl.

One step. Then another and Dad met her at the end of the aisle, linking his arm with hers and holding her hand. Which was super sweet since she was in the middle of something that felt like riding a wave into the side of a building.

"Smile, sweetheart," Dad said, quietly.

She lifted her gaze to Knox's, worried that the sight of him waiting there for her would throw her further off kilter.

But that's not what happened.

Knox winked like they'd talked about. She winked back like they'd planned.

He grinned. She grinned.

Her breaths were ragged as they walked toward him, but she did her best not to look like she'd had extra helpings of beans for lunch.

Somehow they made it to the front of the aisle. She wasn't certain how, since the whole thing was kind of a blur.

"Dearly beloved, we be gathered here today," Bax said in an—on any other day—impressive pirate accent. "t' join this scallywag 'n this wench in matrimony."

Did he really call her a wench?

"Oh God," Courtney said, loud enough for everyone.

Uh-huh. Irina bit at her tongue so she wouldn't say anything, but then she caught Knox's gaze and it didn't matter that Bax talked like a pirate, and she wasn't in character, because she was with Knox.

"You can take a breath," Knox said. "You probably should do that."

Right, breathing was so important. She nodded and did that. Then she did it again.

Knox reached for her hand when her father did the whole, "Her mother and I support her decision to marry this rock star."

The switching of the hands was not part of the plan. But it felt super nice, grounding her in the moment. She let him pull her closer and allowed him to be the stability she needed until she found her sea legs.

"Thank you," she whispered.

He squeezed in response.

Bax continued on with the ceremony she only slightly understood. "When a full-pocketed cur 'n a proud beauty decide t' spend thar lives together, 'tisn't t' be taken lightly…"

They'd most definitely be discussing the ad-libbing later.

"Do ye Jeremy take Irina t' be yer wife?" Bax asked.

"If rum can't fix it, you're not using enough rum," the parrot on his shoulder answered instead of Knox.

"Ignore him," Bax continued. "Just answer my question."

"I do take Irina to be my wife," Knox said, slipping a gold band on her ring finger. Nothing flashy. They'd agreed not to do the flashy jewelry. Originally, because it wasn't like they'd be using it long term. But Irina actually liked that the ring wasn't in-your-face flashy and was more subdued.

"'n do ye Irina take Jeremy t' be yer ol' mate?" Bax continued.

"Ye can have me booty, but leave me chest alone," the parrot answered for her.

That got a solid laugh from the audience. She was just grateful he wasn't cussing or giving sex tips.

"Roger, hush," Bax said out of the corner of his mouth.

Irina side-eyed him, but took the matching gold band from Linx and slid it on Knox's finger. "I do take you to be my husband."

Bax continued the ceremony, still in full-on pirate. He'd seriously committed to this role.

This was a moment where decisions were made. She could either be ticked off that he went so wildly off script, or she could be impressed with his commitment to character and not following directions.

She decided being impressed was the most logical option, since getting mad wouldn't do anyone any good or change anything. The parrot hadn't pooped, either, so there was also that, and Courtney would likely not be angry about it.

"Knox here wrote his wench a chanty. Prepare yer ears," Bax scooted to the side while Tanner handed over a guitar.

"You wrote me a song?" Irina asked, suddenly feeling mighty guilty about the lack of pie she'd prepared for him. She needed to fix that.

Knox grinned, nodded, and strummed.

"Yo ho, yo ho," the parrot started up again.

Knox continued strumming until Bax got the bird to chill. Then laid it on her, piercing her with his stare as he sang.

There's a woman in my mind,
Who always knows just where to be,
She's there and then she's not,
I swear she's everything I need.

"Ohhh…" she said to no one but herself, her cheeks burning for some strange reason.

Her eyes are an enigma,
Her hair is just the same,
But when her lashes drift open,
I know I'll find my way,
She'll lead me all the way.

He continued on about he never knew who she'd be when

she opened her eyes, but he understood no matter who she was, he'd have a helluva time.

Her breath caught and she had to force her lungs to work. This was *her* song. He'd written *her* a love song.

Sure, perhaps she did have a thing for colored contacts, but she didn't realize he'd write an entire song about it. A song with such depth and heart that made her fight tears so she wouldn't cry out the green contact lenses she'd picked to go with the red dress.

He finished and she didn't even care there was a parrot tossing out lines during the ceremony. The guests applauded, but she was only vaguely aware of their presence. Stuck in place, in a time bubble where she wasn't entirely sure what to do, why she was there, or what came next.

She didn't care, either, because right then she was herself and it was perfect. This was life with Knox—random pirates and birds.

Knox handed the guitar back to Tanner and took his place beside her again. She pushed up on her tippy toes when they were back side-to-side.

"I feel like I owe you a monologue or something," she said into his ear.

"Pie," was all he said, raising his eyebrows.

Yes, after that, she owed the man a whole bakery of pies.

"By the power vested in me, by the Church o' the Flying Spaghetti Monster"—Bax leaned into their space, getting way too close with the bird—"That's wha' it's called. Didn' make it up." He leaned back. "I now pronounce ye ol' mate 'n beauty. Ye can kiss if ye wants t'."

She slid her gaze to Knox. He stared at her; head tilted to the side.

One second. Then two.

"Are you going to kiss me or what?" she asked.

He moved in so their mouths were close, but not touching.

"Figured I'd let you kiss me," he said against her lips.

Ugh, the man was amazing and so frustrating all in the same moments.

So she did kiss him. Mostly because that song was phenomenally kickass. Also, because she wanted to and he had most definitely earned it.

Her mouth met his and her whole body both strung tight and relaxed all at the same time. He kissed her back, not being ridiculous about it and opening his mouth for tongue on tongue, but with restraint she wanted to break through. Restraint she wanted to prove she could overpower.

So it was she who parted her lips. She who opened her mouth and tested with her tongue. She who melted into him and didn't come up for air. Because he tasted like spearmint, and smelled of sawdust. And she was one hundred percent off kilter, and he was a life raft. Safety in a sea of sharks.

So, uh-huh, she kissed him. Didn't stop.

The catcalls started, so she probably should've used that as a cue to step away. But all the pent-up *everything* spilled into that kiss.

A tap on her shoulder brought her up from the waves, but she didn't break the kiss.

Neither did he.

"Ye two might wants t' get a cabin," Bax said, still tapping away at her shoulder.

Oh, yes, there were people here watching them. Cameras clicking away. Knox released his grip on her, and she did the same.

Bax had been tapping on both of their shoulders, apparently, because he didn't stop when they quit snogging.

They both shrugged him off, she glanced at Knox from under her wicked-long fake eyelashes. He was grinning a total shit-eating grin.

"Seven-point-eight," he said at the same time she said, "Total ten."

She probably should've removed a few percentage points

since neither of them read the room and paused without intervention.

Yet...

"Seven-point-eight?" She drew her eyebrows together, appalled. No one in the world would rate a kiss like that as a seven-point-eight.

"Better keep practicing," he added with a wink that warmed her to her toes.

"Practice makes perfect," Roger, the parrot, added.

She had a feeling he wasn't wrong.

Chapter Seventeen
KNOX

DESPITE THE FACT Bax had gone rogue with his pirate antics—oh, they'd continued through the reception—Courtney and Irina did not kill him, and Knox only had to referee once. That wasn't even with Bax, that was with the bird.

Honest, if that had been a real wedding with an actual love match, he probably wouldn't have had the kind of fun they'd had. He had a feeling the reason today was so great was... Irina.

He used the keycard to let them into the suite at the Four Seasons where they'd start their honeymoon. Start, and finish, since Irina began rehearsals immediately.

They hadn't needed the bell staff to help with their luggage, as they'd only packed minimally for the night. Not like this was a real honeymoon or anything. Real in the sense they'd just gotten married. Not real in the sense that there was going to be no hanky-panky.

The bags set near the table, he moved to the curtains to look out onto downtown Denver.

He should pick a bedroom and change into sweatpants or

something. Maybe even see if Irina was hungry, and he'd order up room service.

That's what he should do…find a menu. The second-best thing to honeymoon sex was good food. Or so he figured.

"I'm so ready to get out of this thing." Irina came from one of the bedrooms pulling at the bodice of the crimson dress, trying to turn it so she could get to the buttons and having no luck at all.

What was the protocol for something like this? Did he offer to help her get out of her clothes? Was that copacetic?

"Can I get your help?" Irina asked, getting flustered, her cheeks turning red as she still tried to turn the dress and had no luck because her breasts got in the way.

Good to know, the groom helped with this type of thing even when things weren't going further than the bridal extraction.

He stepped up and worked the buttons free one by one.

Unfortunately, being this close to her, alone with her, reminded him of kissing her. He would not allow himself to think of that kiss they'd had to punctuate the ceremony, or how he'd ranked her lower only because he'd been certain she was going to do the same and he worried about his pride.

Honestly? She was correct, it'd been a ten. With Irina things were always a ten. The thought made his throat get fuzzy.

The way she'd melted into him so easily that he'd forgotten where they were, what they were doing, and why they should stop. The fine hairs of his arms stood to attention at only the thought of her mouth on his.

The dress was held together with pearl buttons slipped through a thin layer of some kind of string. While he could play keyboard and guitar like nobody's business, his hands weren't used to trying to unhook teensy little buttons one at a time.

"Damn," he said, fighting with a fifth button. These

babies did not want to release easily. No, they seemed to want to hold her close and not let her go.

He could relate, seeing as she smelled like coconut and vanilla with an extra scoop of cherries.

Her hair was still curled and pinned, but she'd released some of the clips as soon as they hit the hotel room, so some of the locks fell over her shoulders, all the way down to her cleavage. Her eyes had been green earlier; now they were slate gray with blue flecks.

"This is your real eye color?" he asked, working on the next button.

At this rate, they'd be standing there all night.

She nodded and grunted when he pulled the button so it'd give him enough space to release. "Uh-huh."

"I like it." They were the kind of understated pretty that took a guy by surprise.

She shook her head. "Ugh. Really? No."

"Why?"

"They're plain."

They weren't plain. Not at all.

"What was the deal with Linx and Bax?" she asked, pulling off bracelets and unhooking her earrings while he continued to work the buttons free.

"What do you mean?" he asked the question even though he knew precisely what she meant. Linx and Bax took their covert, unsanctioned operation seriously.

She gave him a look like she was about to call him on his bullshit, so he dodged—

"I don't really want to tell you." Damn, these buttons were a pain, how did she get them on in the first place? Right about now he wished this was a real honeymoon so he could pull the buttons free and then use his mouth on her until she forgot, or just didn't care anymore, that he'd fucked up her gown.

"You *have* to tell me." She held the front of the bodice as he worked his way down her back. Who came up with this method of keeping clothing on a person? Whoever it was had a masochistic streak and probably hated sex.

"Why couldn't they just use a zipper like a normal dress?" he asked, under his breath.

"Because it's designer and not off the rack at the mall." She shifted, moving her ass a little in his direction. "Now spill. What was up with your bandmates?"

"They mean well, they just forget to use their boundaries and good judgement sometimes." That was the fucking truth. "That's all."

"What were they doing that they meant well?" She leaned her palms on the dresser, arching her back so he could have a better grasp on one of the middle buttons.

Fine, he'd tell her. It wasn't like she couldn't call her bestie Courtney and get the dirt from her. The guys said they were being covert, but he was fairly certain they didn't know what that meant. Even if they were, Bax was putty in Courtney's hands and that wasn't going to change over a mildly important secret.

Knox put his entire focus on the buttons as he spoke. "The guys like you; they want you to stick around, they're trying to make you permanent."

"I'm not going anywhere."

"I know, but they like the assurance that we're married so you have to stick around."

"That's ridiculous."

He shrugged. "They think we should actually do this thing for real."

Irina stilled.

He didn't like that. Didn't like the feeling that by not moving she'd punched him.

"What do you mean, a real marriage?" she asked, gently and with a whole helping of caution. "We're *really* married. There was *real* paperwork, and a *real* marriage certificate."

He glanced up to the mirror in front of them, her eyes held onto him in the glass. With the way her pupils dilated, and her breaths came quick?

She knew what they meant by a real marriage.

"You want a *real* marriage?" she asked, still staring at mirror Knox. Speaking to him through the glass.

Real in the sense of forever? Probably not.

Real in the sense that once he got the dress off of her they could enjoy each other? Uh...he was human, and she was gorgeous.

He stopped with the buttons, instead running his palms over her shoulders, down to her elbows, and pulling her arms aside so the front of the bodice fell forward the slightest of inches.

She wasn't bare underneath; she had some kind of lingerie there that seriously made him worry he might actually rip her dress to bust her out of the buttons.

Goosebumps trailed along her exposed skin at his touch. They echoed along his own skin as though they shared that connection already and their bodies were in sync.

"I'm not sure." He pressed his lips to the junction where her neck met her shoulder. "Do you?"

Her breathing became jagged. "Maybe you should confirm with me what you mean by real? So I'm clear?"

He'd much rather show her, but he could use his words like a grown-up.

"Well, if we have a real marriage, I guess we'd have a real wedding night. That means I'd take you to bed and make you come so many times the only thing you'd remember would be my name." That about summed up what a real marriage was to him at the present moment.

"This is what Bax and Linx want for us?"

"Bax and Linx have no idea what they want. They just needed something to do."

"What were...uh...their ideas to make this real marriage

happen?" She hit him with a haymaker when she caught his gaze in the mirror.

He spoke to the image of her, because it was easier than turning her to him and speaking directly to the woman he was pretty sure he didn't want to pretend with anymore.

Holding her gaze steady, he said, "To sing to you, cook for you, and then go down on you."

Her eyes widened only the slightest of millimeters. Then a wicked grin traced along her mouth. "So far their plan sounds reasonable."

Did she just? She did just…

"I don't understand you." He didn't. "But I want to."

"Okay, let's say this is a real wedding night," she said, still staring at him through the image in the mirror. "What would come next?"

"Well, I sure as hell would give up on your button situation," he said. Instead of ripping her buttons free, or fighting with them, he started undoing the buttons down the front of his shirt. Testing the waters to see if she'd stop him. "So I could start undressing myself."

She didn't stop him.

Didn't ask him to stop.

"Knox," she said his name like a request. He wasn't sure what request she was making, however.

"Would you like me to continue undoing my shirt?" he asked. "If this were real?"

She nodded, her throat clearly thick. "Yes."

"I like you, Irina." He continued with the buttons since these were a helluva lot easier to undo than the ones on her dress. "Real or not."

They stared at each other in the mirror for a long beat, until something changed in her expression. A warmth shone through like a candle that had been lit long enough to really melt the wax and not just burn the wick.

"If this were real then I'd start touching you," she said.

"Then maybe you should do that?" His words were rough against his vocal cords.

She pulled her bottom lip between her teeth, nodded, and turned to him, moving her hands to his lapel and then brushing his fingers aside to finish the buttons herself.

"I like you, too," she whispered, her hands moving to the belt at his waistband, unlocking it.

Now that was an invitation if he'd ever had one.

"Then what are we doing here?" he asked, his body already getting ideas as to what it wanted to do with her, even as his hands moved to her jaw, brushed along her cheekbone, and dove into her hair.

"Well, if this was a real wedding night, it sounds like you'd sing me a song and then go down on me." She said this like it was a joke, but the little wobble to her voice told him there was more to it. This wasn't funny, and it wasn't a joke. "You already did the cooking part."

She reached for the collar of his open shirt, pulling him closer so his mouth was right near hers. This wasn't for a show, this was just for them. "Or maybe you'd prefer I go down on you instead?"

He had a hard time forming a thought, what with all the blood rushing to a particular appendage at the thought of her mouth there.

"I'd have to ask you a question, and it's a serious one," he managed to say.

"Ask away," she whispered, kissing his collarbone, moving down to his pecs, and kissing a trail all the way past his belly button until she was on her knees.

He inhaled a sharp breath, because he wanted to be a good guy for her. "Did you have a whole lot of the champagne fountain tonight? Hypothetically? Or some of those leftover cucumber sandwiches?"

She laughed, her chest heaving against his body, her mouth pausing just at his waistband. "No. I am not drunk."

"If this were real, I'd be incredibly turned on right now." Though that much was clear with his pants around his ankles.

"If this were real," she said, looking up at him. "I'd be very impressed."

The night went a little fuzzy at that point, because she opened her mouth and drew him in. If this wasn't real, he didn't want to wake up.

He groaned, his hands in her hair, her mouth working his erection.

Irina knew how to use her mouth. Not that he'd questioned it, but holy shit did she know how to add a sweep of the tongue that nearly made him embarrass himself.

While he wasn't a guy to ever turn down a blow job from a gorgeous woman, if they were doing this—and it seriously seemed like they were doing this—he wasn't going to lose his load before she got her cookies.

"Noodle Cup," he whispered, a lot jagged because she used that moment to do a sweep and turn with her lips that made his words rough. "Your turn first," he managed to say.

She continued working him, making a nuh-uh sound against his flesh.

Gently, he reached down to stroke her cheek. "Stand up, Irina."

She did stand, reached for his hand, and ran it along the side of her breast, down past her waist to her hip. Since he was there and she was offering, he grabbed a handful of ass, pulling the length of her to the front of him.

His heart beat faster, his breaths came uneven, and the erection he'd been nursing since he saw her in that dress pulsed between them.

Generally, he liked to take control when it came to all things sex. Not to say he was a professional—he'd never been paid in anything other than baked goods—but he knew what he liked and knew what needed to be done to get everyone involved to a climax or two.

At the moment, however, his mind went blank.

"How are we going to get me out of this dress?" She quirked an eyebrow, sultry and every inch the vixen.

"I have a thought." He ran his hands down her back to the spot where he'd stopped with the buttons. He gave a little tug there to illustrate that thought.

"It's not like I'm going to wear it again." She seemed to dare him with a look.

What the hell, they were doing this, might as well make it memorable.

He pulled the halves apart, buttons pinging wood and mirror as they bounced off the furniture.

With only the littlest assist from him, Irina stepped from the gown, and he got his first look at the lingerie he wasn't supposed to see.

Fuuuck, she was perfection.

Chapter Eighteen
IRINA

THERE WERE times when a girl appreciated the designer flourishes on a gown, and a time when she wished they'd used snaps instead. Today was the second option.

Though she'd never had a fantasy of a man ripping her dress from her body, turns out that was precisely the kind of fantasy she should've been having all these years.

Knox's He-Man antics did it for her. Oh boy, did they do it.

There was a moment when the dress fell to the ground and she thought he might actually devour her. The way his eyes scraped across every inch of her skin turned her on in ways she'd never known. Made her wet and want and not even care that he was her husband, and this could complicate *everything*.

Honestly, she had a hard time getting that turned on without a battery-operated assist. But who didn't?

With the dress out of the way, there were hands and mouths everywhere and no one even needed to consider running to Battery Mart for anything. The place between her thighs pulsed with needs that Knox's body currently made promises to fulfill. She hoped like hell he was a follow-througher and not an over-promiser and under-deliverer.

They came together in what seemed to be a well-choreographed salsa to the bed.

He wasn't demanding in the bedroom, but he clearly didn't mind taking the lead, and he understood how to turn every nerve ending on her body to high alert. The high alert bit wasn't due to any *one* thing, but rather a whole slew of movements, sounds, and attention. A whole sensory experience.

The man was all attentive. She moaned, he followed through. She groaned, he explored.

And, he actually did sing to her, low and rough. Some Bryan Adams song she recognized, but couldn't quite put the title to because he stopped singing when his mouth fell between her legs. Stopped singing and started using that mouth for other things.

She'd never had a Bryan Adams fantasy before either. Shoulda been doing that, too. All this time and her fantasies had never hit the mark.

He found her sweet spot on the first try—something even she had a hard time mastering. But there he was, his mouth and hands bringing her to climax before she could even register what was happening or where Bryan Adams ever ended up.

Her breasts heaved, she made noises that usually only happened when she handled things herself. Not that she'd had tons of guys take her to bed, but enough that she sort of figured they all had no idea what the hell they were doing.

Turns out, she'd been meeting the wrong men.

Because they weren't Knox and his skills with his—

"How did you just do that?" Her hands bunched in the sheets and her heels pressed into the mattress as she built up again.

Before she could take a tumble down orgasm mountain

again, Knox wasn't there anymore. He hustled to his pants, removed his wallet, grabbed a condom, and then he was back. Lickety-banana-split, the condom was in position, and she parted her legs for him.

"If this were real," she said, when he moved over the top of her. "That would be the most amazing orgasm of my life."

"Tell me more about this orgasm?" he asked, as he entered her body one small bit at a time.

Her internal muscles already primed for another tumble, she gripped his shoulders and guided him home. "I didn't even need to get my special lipstick."

Fully seated inside her, he moved, thrust, used his hips and made a swirl motion that made her eyes roll back in her head. In a good way.

"What does this lipstick do?" he asked, slowing a little, but not so much she had to urge him on. More like a turn around the corner of a back road, you had to slow down to get where you wanted to go.

"It's my battery-operated lipstick that I use to…you know." She pressed her palms into his back because he did the hip dip and swirl thing that nudged right against her G-spot.

"You take this lipstick with you wherever you go?" he asked, way too interested in a lipstick she was pretty certain she didn't need ever again.

"No!" Her body was putty in his hands, her ability to think rationally was utterly screwed. That's the only explanation as to why she'd told him about her special lipstick tube. "Not everywhere."

A wry grin came across his lips as he continued his full advance on her senses.

"Just on our honeymoon," she said. "When I wasn't expecting to get any."

"You have this lipstick here?" he confirmed.

"Uh-huh," she said, even as his tempo shifted and he really got into his groove.

She arched her back a little extra so he could go deeper. That got her a moan from the back of his throat.

"Knox," she said his name as a third wave began its cascade through her. "Knox."

His lips came to her ear, and he whispered nonsensical words that instantly had her body relaxing into his, the coil inside cinching tighter.

"Now," he said, completing a full hip dip and thrust at precisely the correct angle for her body to peak and spasm around him.

"Fuuuck," he said, as her muscles tensed and then relaxed.

Clearly the guy had been paying attention in sex education class, because there was no way he learned that on the streets.

They both breathed heavy, spent and sated. Gah, she could sleep for days after that kind of a release.

Though, she had a feeling given her new knowledge of Knox's bedroom skills, she wouldn't be getting a whole lot of sleep that night.

Her breaths finally evening out, she reached for his hand, pulling it to her lips.

"Ten," she said. "Maybe even an eleven because you got bonus points for the extra credit."

He chuckled. "Who knew a honeymoon could be so fun?"

This thing between them wasn't the least bit awkward. It should've been awkward given that they'd just violated all of the rules they'd agreed on when they started this journey together. He pressed light kisses to her cheeks, nose, and throat. "Go get it."

"I just told you, I didn't need it."

"And I just found out we get to *play*."

"Knox." He couldn't be serious. Could he?

Given the glint in his eye? Totally serious.

"After we're done?" he asked, his hands starting to wander.

"Yes?"

He pressed the tip of his nose to hers. "We're gonna sleep."

"Okay," she agreed. Because she had a feeling they'd both need it if he got out her special battery-operated lipstick tube.

"And after that?" he asked, toying with the side of her breast.

"Uh-huh?"

"I'm gonna take you on a real honeymoon." He pressed a kiss to her nipple, licking there and then blowing on it.

"Oh yeah?" How was she so turned on again already? They'd *just* had sex.

Scratch that. How was he so turned on again already? If she wasn't mistaken—and she wasn't mistaken—his lower body was ready to be back in the game.

"I thought we covered this. I can't go to the beach since I've got to be here," she said, running her thigh between his legs, along the shaft of his erection.

"Not the islands." He shook his head. "Oh no. Noodle Cup, I'm taking you to a bagel shop."

She laughed as he rolled her to her back and took over again.

Leave it to Knox to know precisely what she needed.

She was not going to process that she'd had the most amazing sex of her life with...*her husband.*

Chapter Nineteen
KNOX

THE LAST THING Knox wanted was to go back to reality, where he slept alone, made music, and took random online courses at night.

But nights like last night, with Irina, were not in his future. They couldn't be. He got that. Didn't mean he didn't want a repeat. As a partner, Irina was sturdy, responsive, and giving, and…that mouth of hers did things…things he enjoyed…*yeah*.

"You're going to have to look at this eventually," Irina said, flipping through her cell.

At some point she'd gotten up out of bed and put on underwear and a tight white T-shirt. He didn't like that because he wasn't done playing.

Oh hell yes, they'd played. And played. Like five times, they'd played.

No bra, so her nipples at least showed through. There was that.

He, however, was a man of least resistance, so he didn't get dressed at all. Clothes were way too confining when a girl brought her vibrating lipstick tube to bed.

"They're talking about the wedding." She continued flipping, eyes on her cell. Which was stupid, because later they had to go back to their lives and there were people in their lives. People who would interrupt.

She sighed.

He didn't like that sigh.

"You should put the phone down and climb on top," he suggested.

"How many times can you actually have sex in twelve hours?" she asked, clearly not aware that he had serious stamina when it came to this kind of thing.

"I think we should find out." He kissed her arm.

"Knox." She tossed the phone on the nightstand. "We are going to have to talk about what happened last night. And you are going to have to address the baby delivery. It's totally taking precedence over our wedding." She lay alongside him, face to face, but with space between their bodies.

Since she was there, he placed his hand on her hip and rubbed circles there with his thumb. His body may have been tired from all the activity, but he wasn't dead, so his dick stirred.

"What happened last night was we had some pretty epic sex." He nuzzled her neck.

She chuckled, touched his jaw in a way he hadn't realized he enjoyed so much. "Yeah. Epic."

"On the other issue? I'm not talking about it. It'll go away if I don't address it." As did most things in life, except his parents.

"See, you'd think that. But now they got to Craig and Cathy. They're trying to get to me through my agent, my e-mail…everything."

His stomach felt a little funny at that, and for the first time in his life the prospect of sex didn't sound fun. "You gonna talk to them? Tabloids?"

"No, of course not." She shook her head. "But you should."

Unfortunately, this conversation was totally wrecking his libido. He rolled on his back, hand to his forehead.

He didn't want to address it. Was he glad he'd delivered the kid? Yeah, because no one else was there to do it. Sort of like an alone-in-the-shower hand job. Sometimes he just had to handle things. Didn't make him a hero.

Irina didn't let him slip away into his own head; she did a press-up over the top of him. But since her arms weren't so long, mostly her breasts were all up in his grill.

He didn't mind.

"You are not an asshole," she whispered against his mouth, wriggling her body down so the core of her lined up with his erection.

"Well, that's debatable." He swallowed hard against the thoughts of things written about him.

"No." She wriggled more. "What I mean is, in the eyes of everyone out there, you are not an asshole. You are Knox and you have great taste in women." She kissed his lips. "That's me." She spread her legs and sat up, so without the barrier of her panties, she'd be riding him cowgirl.

See? That was exactly the problem with putting on clothes in the middle of the honeymoon.

"You're also good in an emergency sitch," she reached down to pull off her tee. Now, that's what he was talking about. "So you should embrace that, own it."

"Are you trying to get your way by showing me your boobs?" Because it was working. She had great boobs. Big handfuls of breasts that made him reconsider being an ass man.

He used the backs of his hands to trace along the swell of her breasts, over the edges, down to her navel, then back up. "You wanted to talk about something? I can talk for a while."

"Look how chatty you get when you have something to play with," she said, pulling his hands to the front so they were at her nipples.

He'd never been so aroused during an important conversation before.

"I'm listening," he said, even as he lifted himself up to give a little lick and pinch to the right nipple.

She pushed him back down. "Now, while I have your attention, we do need to talk, because we did have sex."

"Had is in the past and it appears we're about to do it again." He cupped his hands behind his skull so he wouldn't be totally distracted by her breasts. "So we need to talk because we are actively having sex."

"What does it mean for us?" she asked, as cautious as a woman could with her breasts on display.

She had a little freckle there on the left one, right beside the pink nipple. "Means we're both going to be in an excellent mood when we go have bagels."

She chewed at her bottom lip. "Be serious."

"I am being serious." He took everything they discussed seriously.

"Knox." The way she said his name made him stop with the mouth-on-nipple tug. Which was hard given that her core was rubbing against his erection and that meant there wasn't a full blood supply to his brain.

"What do you want it to mean?" he asked, genuinely, moving his thumb to pull her bottom lip from between her teeth.

"I don't know," she whispered, and shook her head. The sort of wrecked expression on her face brought him up cold.

Instead of continuing the conversation with her rack in his face, he adjusted himself and pulled her down on top, her forehead to his collarbone. Her hands were against his shoulders. If they hadn't just spent all night making each other come, and he wasn't totally naked, it might have passed as platonic.

"I don't know, either," he admitted to the top of her head. "But I know I want to do it again."

"With just me?" she asked.

There were times when he didn't really understand what was happening around him. Like the time at the Olive Garden when they'd asked if he wanted soup or salad and he thought they meant a Super Salad and he said yes. But that wasn't what they meant.

"I guess not?" she frowned.

"I'm not saying no. It's just I didn't expect this."

"Expect exclusivity?"

Ohhhh. That made more sense. "I thought you were offering up a threesome. Sorry. My bad."

She smacked his shoulder, light and playful.

"Simmer down there, Knox. I mean, are we going to be exclusive?" She enunciated each word, but it wasn't necessary. He understood now.

"I'm going to be totally honest here," he said. "Last night was amazing." He touched her bottom lip with his thumb, held her gaze with his. "I like you. I like you a lot. I don't think about anyone else except you. Wondering what you're doing and where you're at. I don't know what that means because I haven't had this experience before. But I know the thought of another guy touching you makes me want to keep you right here and feed you bagels. So, yeah, I think if we're gonna keep doing this? I'd appreciate if we didn't do it with other people, sanctity of marriage and keeping you all to myself."

She let out what seemed to be a relieved breath. "I like that."

"I'm not promising you forever," he said. Clarifying for her or him or maybe both of them? "Because I don't know how to do that, but I can promise you right now."

"So we just write an amendment to our agreement."

"Does it have to be on paper? Because that sounds like I'm not going to enjoy it."

"No." She shook her head. "Just that we'll ride this out until it's time to stop."

He could be on board with that.

"You wanna come on the tour with me?" he asked, and then a boulder tumbled in his stomach because he'd never asked anyone to come with him before. She might say no. That wouldn't be awesome. "When your gig here is done," he clarified. "You could come along." He paused. "If you wanted."

"So you can feed me bagels?" She pressed her breasts against him, and it didn't seem to be to start anything, but here he was starting to lose brain blood flow.

"So we can bang and then I can feed you bagels," he said, moving his hand between her legs.

She parted her thighs, letting him touch her there. "Once this show's done, I could seriously use a break."

"Then come with me on tour." He moved his thumb over the bundle of nerves he'd discovered around two a.m. made her very agreeable.

"I'll think about it," she said on a gasp.

He moved one finger inside, then two. "Stop thinking and let's do it."

"You just want me to put out regularly," she said as she moved against his hand, finding a rhythm together.

"I want to be with you, Noodle Cup." He pressed a kiss to the tip of her nose. "Let's just have some fun together."

"I want to be with you, too, Knox." She moaned, her head pressing deeper into the pillow. "Fun sounds amazing."

"See? Everyone gets what they want, and everyone ends up happy." He did the index finger, pinky thing that drove her over the edge.

Judging by her rapid breaths, she was nearly there. Honestly, he might *not* need an assist to follow her.

"You're so weird," she murmured, relaxing and making total sex sounds as the orgasm took hold.

"And you love it." He grunted, pressed the long hard length of himself against her thigh, reveling in the sensation of her internal muscles pulsing around his hand. "Because a wise woman told me once that compromises are the key to any successful marriage."

Chapter Twenty
KNOX

WEEKS WENT by like hours when a guy was having a good time.

The one life lesson that Knox learned when he was a preteen and his parents announced their divorce: when things are great like this, you have to prepare for the pivot because they're about to go to shit.

"I have a little something to show you." He bounced on the bedspread next to Irina. Where she read through a new script. She seemed to get them all the time.

Today there was no production, so she lounged in jeans and his vintage KISS tee. The one with Gene Simmons on the front.

They didn't check out of the Four Seasons, they just extended their stay until his house was finished so they could be alone. The house still wasn't complete, which sucked because she hadn't been able to bake him pie. But was fine, because Irina spent tons of time at the theater—he'd seen the show, she was phenomenal. He didn't love the way her character pined for this Sergio, but he also got that it wasn't Irina up there. It was all her talent shining through, and he was so damn proud.

"You need a minute or are you at a stopping point?" he asked.

"Stopping point." She flipped the script closed and stood, stretching.

Something was off with her, but he couldn't quite put his finger on it. Nothing obvious, just the way her grin hadn't met her eyes, and she didn't linger on his gaze, touch his arm. Shit like that.

"Follow me," he said, slipping on his shoes and heading out.

Her career was on pointe, and he was not the asshole anymore. The plan had worked. The tabloids let up on him and moved their attention to Mach, calling him the new Dimefront asshole.

Mach loved it. Loved the attention and the groupies who wanted to be with the bad boy of the group. He played up the role just fine.

On top of it all, the tour was coming up. With Irina agreeing to come along, wanting to come along and looking forward to the European portion so she could eat Belgian waffles and chocolate croissants with him, they'd started planning.

The giddy feelings he got around her kept getting bigger, better, and he sort of forgot this wasn't a match they'd picked themselves.

"What's up?" she asked, following him.

"Come with me." He reached for her hand. Kissed her, because he could, and then loaded her up in his sedan and drove her to his house. Their house.

The house that no one else would live in but them.

Hand on the doorknob, he asked, "Are you ready?"

"What are you talking about?" she asked as he pushed open the door. Then her eyes went wide, like his had when he first saw it.

"Oh, hells yes, it's not pink." She squeed, gripped his arm.

"Do you smell that?" he asked, making an exaggerated sniff sound.

"Smell what?" She sniffed, rather daintily.

"That's what I'm talking about." He clapped his hands like he was giving the room a standing ovation. "It doesn't stink anymore in here."

Yeah, everything was coming up Knox.

"This is so great." Irina did a twirl in the living room. "You must be so freaking excited."

Something sat funny with the way she said *you* and not *we*.

"One more thing." He reached for her hand and pulled her with him through the house to the primary suite. The room he'd changed course on in the past few weeks. Once the carpet came in, he'd made some changes. Hired a decorator to put things together. Given direction while she was at work, approved sketches, and appreciated the finished product.

They got to the door and his heart beat a little faster than it should've, since this was sort of for her. He wanted her to like it.

"Close your eyes," he said.

She did.

He pushed open the door.

"Open them," he said, a little frog lodging in his larynx.

She opened and gasped. "Holy crap, this looks amazing."

Early on when she'd been helping him pick out fixtures and carpet, they'd had a bit of a tiff over the color of bedroom carpet. She'd insisted on neutral gray. He preferred bachelor black.

However, since they'd be spending lots of time in the space—preferably naked time—he took her suggestion.

He also had the whole thing decorated with remote opening curtains, a big-ass bed with high-thread count sheets, solid-wood dressers, and two giant closets. He hadn't filled them with clothes for her, but only because Irina had her own style, and he had a hunch she'd want to do it herself and not use a personal shopper.

She let out a huge breath. "This is amazing. It turned out fabulous." She gave him a knowing grin. "Aren't you glad you went with gray? I told you it'd look amazing."

"My closet is over here. Your closet is over there." He gestured to her side. "Two en suite baths means twice the fun." Especially the shower in her bathroom with the four shower heads? Oh, yeah, he had plans for those.

"My closet?" she asked, moving toward the little room that wasn't so little.

He'd had the decorator add lots of space for Irina's shoe collection and extra shelving for handbags he'd realized she had a bit of a crush on.

"Yeah, I figured you'd want a place to put your clothes." Made sense to him.

He rocked back and forth, toe to heel. Toe to heel. This wasn't quite the reaction he'd expected. The whole frowny thing going on with her.

"Knox." She pulled her lips together in a way he hadn't ever seen her do before. "I…uh…do you want me to move in?"

Uh…yes?

"Well, seeing as we are married and you and I sleep in the same bed every night, I figured…" Where had he missed the cues that she wouldn't expect to be sharing his space?

"Oh." That's all she said. Just, oh.

He had a pretty tough skin, but that one stung.

"Irina, I think I may have read things wrong. You don't want to move in?" he asked. "I got your color for carpet." That sounded slightly pathetic, didn't it?

"I think we should've talked about it before you put in gray carpet," she said quickly.

"I'm confused." He lifted his hands, and did not enjoy the

way his skin felt too tight. "Because we agreed to be exclusive. We've been going at it like it's our job. And you're going on tour with me. I figured I'd make you comfortable."

"Okay, um…" She sat on the cuddle chair in the reading nook he'd added to the side of the room by her closet. The one he figured she could lounge on to read her scripts. She ran her hands through her hair. She'd dyed it brown for the role of Persephone.

He didn't like the direction of this conversation. Didn't enjoy the way his ears had that odd rushing sound and he wanted to go outside, find a busy street, and count cars.

"You know how we agreed to tell each other when something important happens?" she asked.

He nodded.

"I got an offer." Her eyes were a little red when she said this. "I want to take it. It's uh…a big one. I'm a key actress. They'll put my name on the poster at the theaters. Right in the middle next to Chris Hemsworth. Only a tiny bit smaller." Her words got breathier as she spoke. Her chest raising and falling like she was about to cry.

She didn't need to cry. Because… "That's amazing. Fantastic. Champagne fountain worthy."

She nodded. "Yeah, uh…"

A tear fell out of the corner of her eye.

Nope, he didn't like that. He crouched in front of her at the cuddle chair. "Irina, talk to me."

"Filming's during the tour," she whispered like she didn't really want him to hear.

"Okay, so you can't make the whole thing." The tour lasted like six months, so she'd have time to do both. "You'll work around it."

She did not have the expression of a woman ready to work around anything.

"I can't come, Knox," she said. "I'm going to be filming and then the press junket for the Clooney movie. I can't come." The words seemed to stick in her throat as she spoke, which was apt because they also stuck funny in his ears.

"So you can't come. We'll see each other sometimes. I'll come to you when we've got a break. We get breaks." Not long breaks, and they'd be in Europe so he couldn't just drive over.

She nodded. "I…uh…how are we going to do this?"

"Do you want to keep going forward?" he asked, numbness taking over.

She gulped. "I can't ask you to wait for me."

"What if we wait for each other? It's not always going to be tours and filming. We can find time to be together." Unless they couldn't, but he wasn't ready to accept that yet.

"You really want to keep going?" she asked, and he swore to fuck her words sounded like hope felt.

He nodded. "I'm not done. Are you kidding? I haven't even showed you what I can do with Twizzlers and few glow sticks."

That was some seriously next-level epic. He didn't think she'd be ready for it yet.

She laughed out a breath, but she didn't smile. Wasn't her sunshine self. "I think you're pretty awesome, Knox."

He reached for her jaw. "I also think you are awesome, Noodle Cup."

She laughed again.

He dug the laugh, didn't love the spark that'd left her eyes.

Didn't enjoy the boulder on his chest or the way the world seemed to have started spinning the other direction.

"Tell me about the movie," he said, hoping the excitement of the job would make her smile again, put things to right.

So she did. She sat there on the snuggly chair he'd picked out for her, and told him all about her starring role and what it meant for her. What it meant for her future. Her career. How things were looking up for her.

And while things looked up, for some reason he had the

feeling he was falling. Not a good amusement park falling, but the kind that hurt when a guy finally hit the bottom.

Chapter Twenty-One
IRINA

1 Month Later

THE DUSTY SET was not her favorite place. But she enjoyed all she'd learned about being a lead on a high-level production. People called her Ms. Carmichael instead of "you there!" She had her own trailer that came with a mini fridge. Her assistant—she got one!—Terri, was super sweet and helped her run lines when she needed.

Where Irina preferred bright colors and loads of prints, Terri seemed to have stock in Lululemon. Always going for comfort, always looking like she could assist on set or hit the gym. Irina figured this was the balance she needed in an assistant. Terri could hit the gym and dress in yoga pants, she'd eat cookies and wear bright prints.

"Knox called," Terri said, catching Irina as soon as she stepped from the soundstage. "I told him you were on set until five. We did the math. He'll be onstage right about now. So he suggested you text when you're around and he'll call you back."

This was the story of their lives right now. The whole

"call you back" bit. Irina did her best not to let it get her down, but dammit, she missed him.

"Thanks." Irina grabbed the envelope from Terri. It held the call sheets for the next day and gave her something to focus on instead of missing her husband.

Oh boy, she missed him a freaking lot.

"Knox also sent you this," Terri said, singsong, as she held out a red velvet-wrapped box with a big-ass gold bow.

Irina knew what was in the box, but that didn't matter. She pulled the lid off and grinned. He'd sent her a Cup o' Noodles.

Some guys sent flowers, but they weren't as sweet as Knox and his daily delivery of noodle cups.

In return, she talked dirty to him whenever he wanted her to, and she sent him a pie at every venue. Not homemade, since she wasn't there to make it, but they were both doing their best.

Generally, she kept herself busy so she didn't think about him or what he might be doing. Went to lots of Los Angeles parties she'd never been invited to before. Her picture came up regularly on the tabloid sites in the best ways, making her scoot on up the Hollywood list pretty dang quickly.

But at night when it was just her, and the room was quiet, the noodle cup finished, she curled up in a ball and she cried. Let the tears flow, because dammit, even with her mom and dad stopping by every other day and all the naked models in her living room…she was lonely. The kind of lonely only one person—Knox—could fix.

"Stunt director wants to talk to you about the mountain scene. He's thinking you might want to go with a double? I told him I'd ask," Terri continued, setting the pace for their trek back through the sets and racks of costumes to Irina's little trailer, where she'd change and get ready for another night without Knox.

She frowned at that, because that's what she did these days when she thought about how much she missed the guy.

"Nah, I wanna do that stunt myself." She flipped through the call sheet folder, her box of noodles tucked under her other arm. Not every day a girl got to pretend to climb a mountain with one of the Hemsworth boys.

Her character on set wore blue jeans and those super tight shirts with a low, low, low neckline, so that's what she was wearing. And bright-pink cowgirl boots, since her character was kind of awesome. She sort of hoped the producers would let her keep the boots when filming stopped.

That thought didn't make her smile. Nothing seemed to do that these days—except the noodle deliveries from Knox. It didn't make sense, because this was the life she'd dreamed of since she'd started playing games of pretend. All her dreams were coming true.

So why did she feel so sad all the time?

"What are you doing later?" she asked Terri. "Want to get dressed up and hit the town with *moi*?"

Terri grinned. "Always, but we can't tonight."

Oh, so Terri had plans. Irina waggled her eyebrows. "What kind of plans do *you* have?"

At least needling them out of her new friend would give her something to distract her from missing her guy.

"I don't have plans, but you do." Terri tilted her head toward the trailer, and there, leaning against the door, was her bestest best friend, Courtney.

"You're here," Irina rushed to her friend and met her for a hug. "I've missed you so dang much."

"I brought you a present," Courtney said against her hair when Irina didn't release her right away.

"Gimme." Irina stepped back, making grabby hands.

"I left it inside," Courtney said, a wicked grin on her face.

Irina's heart lodged in her throat as she pulled open the door to her little trailer.

There, lounging on the little sofa, was her husband, in his standard jeans and what she already knew was a super soft T-shirt.

"I have strict orders from Hans to return him to the airport in exactly eight hours," Courtney said. "Make it count."

"Have fun," Terri said, happily closing the door behind Irina.

"How are you not onstage right now?" Irina stood still, unable to move because this could not be happening.

"I missed my wife," he said, standing and stalking in her direction.

She put her call sheets and the box of noodles down, then she threw herself at him.

He met her embrace and kissed the stuffing right out of her.

"Called in a sub so I could fly here to see my girl." His hands were in her hair and his mouth against hers. "Officially, I have the flu."

"That sucks," she said against his mouth. "I think I caught it, too."

"Bummer," he said, his hands everywhere but at his sides.

They were frantic, but the puzzle pieces of who they were when they were alone slipped together without effort. She wasn't only Irina, and he wasn't simply Knox. They were *them*.

"You'll disappoint the fans if you're not there," she said, barely moving her mouth from his and pulling at his shirt.

"They'll live. Rest and recover, that's what the doctor said." He lifted her and wrapped her legs around his waist, planting kisses at her neck as he pressed his erection against her core. Sure, there was loads of clothing between them but just the scent of him, the taste of him, and a small dose of him had her ready to come without any true intimate contact.

"I sent you pie at the arena tonight," she said, out of

breath and grabbing at his ass. "From a restaurant that is apparently awesome."

"Thanks," he said, going straight for her fly. "What kind?"

"Key lime," she said, slanting her mouth to take the kiss deeper.

There was moaning and lots of noises as they pulled at clothing and released a month of pent-up sexual tension.

"What are you going to do while you're here?" she asked, panting as he continued thrusting against her without any regard for rug burn.

"You," he said, moving her to the little space on the floor and coming over the top of her body.

Here's the thing, there wasn't a lot of room in the trailer, and she wasn't petite. Knox wasn't a small guy either, so they were sort of sandwiched there in the small space. But you know what? It worked. They totally made it work.

Chapter Twenty-Two
KNOX

2 Weeks Later

HIS PHONE RANG, and he stepped right out of the VIP meet and greet line to answer.

"Noodle Cup?" he asked. He gestured to their manager, Hans, that he'd be taking a breather.

Hans nodded, he knew the drill.

"Hey," she said. "I caught you." Her voice sounded funny, clogged a little with emotion.

"You okay?" He ducked his head, so she'd have his whole focus. "What's going on?"

"I just…" Her breath shuddered a little. "I needed to hear your voice."

"Bad day at work?" he asked, nodding to Bax as he slipped by, because this call was going to take longer than a few clicks.

She cleared her throat. "I fudged a few lines. We had to do four takes because of me."

"We all have off days," he said. "You're human. Is your mom painting at your apartment today?" He didn't want her to be alone. Not when she sounded like she needed someone to fix her pasta.

"No," she said. "She and Dad decided to go to Yosemite to paint the trees." She stopped. "Not the actual trees, but to do some acrylic or oils or something."

"So you're there all by yourself?" he asked, his throat sounding raspy.

"Uh-huh," she said with a sigh.

"My wife had a bad day and now she's lonely." He hated that he wasn't there to make it better. She needed more than only his voice, she needed to know how damn much he missed her too.

"My hand is at your navel," he said, already striding back to the tour bus so he could talk to his wife in private. "Pushing down under the waistband of your underwear."

"Knox?" she asked, his name uncertain. "Are you still in the VIP line?"

"Nope." He jogged across the little path to the tour buses.

"The pink ones you liked last time," she said with a laugh.

He did like those because there was not a lot of fabric for him to fight with. The second he saw her name flash on the screen of his phone he was hard for her. The moment he heard her voice his dick jolted and begged for attention. But the moment he realized she needed him, too, he was ready to do anything for her.

"I'm on my bus now," he said as he stepped onto the bus and headed for the bedroom. You know, in case somebody came searching for him and heard a conversation they didn't expect. "Put your hands between your legs for me, Noodle Cup."

"Knox," she said, like she was going to balk at his proposal.

"Let me take care of you," he said. "Distract you."

"Are *your* pants still on?" she asked, already breathing hard.

They were on a time crunch, so he didn't even remove his boots. Just unhooked his belt, pulled his pants and his boxers to his thighs, and gripped himself with his right hand.

"Nope," he said, giving his dick a stroke and pull.

"My underwear is off," she said on a breath.

"You wanna video call?" He lay back on the bed, letting his hand pull lazy against his erection.

"Honestly? I just needed to hear your voice before I crash." She sounded spent. "But now I'm all kinds of turned on."

"You want me to sing to you?" he asked, because he would. He'd sing to her all night if that's what she needed, because at some point he'd finally recognized that he'd fallen headfirst in love with this woman.

"Always," she said, making the little noise she always did when he slid his fingers inside her.

"Here's what you're going to do," he said, closing his eyes and picturing her on her bed with her hand between her legs. "Is your lipstick tube nearby?"

She full-on laughed at that. "When is it not?"

"Then let's improvise, yeah?" Improvising could be fun, too.

"I like that," she murmured.

"Put a pillow under your hips, yeah?" he instructed, voice low, sitting up to grab the lotion for himself. "That done?"

There was shuffling in the background before she said, breathy, "Uh-huh."

"My dick is in my hand," he said, because it totally was. "But I wish it was in you."

"Gah, me too." She panted. "I'm using my fingers instead."

"Turn on your lipstick to the first setting," he sang the words, giving himself a dry stroke while she moaned into the mouthpiece. "Put it between your legs in that spot I know you love," he made up the tune as he went along.

"What are you doing?" she asked, breathier than before. "Are you participating?"

"You know I am." He squirted some of the lotion he'd swiped from her bathroom in his palm. Was he an ass for stealing her lotion? Probably. But it smelled like her, and got him off better than his standard. "My dick misses you, but tonight it's not about him. It's about you so you can get to sleep."

"Knox," she said his name in that way she did right before she finished.

"I'm with you and I'm turning it to the next setting, using my fingers with the vibration," he said. "Be a good girl and help me out, yeah?"

The low buzz in the background got louder.

"That's my girl," he said, stroking himself and squeezing a little at the tip.

She made a low rumble noise she always did when he got her there, so he increased the speed of his hand, letting her sounds help him finish. He wasn't ashamed that he also made noises when he came, a growl of her name on his lips as he finished.

"Next time let's FaceTime," she said with a low chuckle.

He'd caught his load in a washcloth and tossed it to the bin. "Think you can sleep now?"

"I miss you, Knox," she said, softly.

"Same," he said, pulling his pants back up and buttoning them. "Need to see you soon, Noodle Cup."

"Next week."

Next week they took a break from filming for some awards show. She'd announced she'd meet them on the coast in Spain.

The timing worked because he only had about a week of lotion left before he totally ran dry.

"A week," he murmured.

"Thank you," she said, the yawn evident in her voice.

"Here for you," he replied. "Always here for you."

"Same," she said. "G'night, Knox."

"Get some sleep, Noodle Cup." He turned off his phone, stood, and let out a long breath.

Then he checked to be sure he was decent, and headed back to the meet and greet.

Chapter Twenty-Three
IRINA

4 Days Later

CALLING Knox to help her get to sleep had become something of a routine. But, really, he did not seem to mind. And even if he sang her the dictionary, she'd call him every night.

But tonight she didn't have to, because she'd finished filming early and hopped on a plane to meet him in France. Her turn to surprise him, she'd decked herself out in one of the Knox sweatshirts they sold outside the shows. The one with his face all over the front.

Then she got in line with Becca and waited her turn.

"He's gonna lose his mind," Becca said, looping her arm with Irina's. "All he does is talk about you. What you're doing. What kind of pie you sent that day."

They nearly made it to the end of the line, she could see him now chatting it up with fans, signing things, and giving Tanner a load of shit about something. Her heart thu-thunked in her chest.

"Time to put the plan in action," Becca whispered.

Irina nodded, pulled out her phone, and dialed his number.

She frowned as she went straight to voicemail.

She turned off the call, her heart sinking a little that he hadn't picked up right away. This would've been better if he picked up like she'd planned.

Fudge. She'd just have to go with plan B.

But just as she started to dial Bax, the current slew of fans moved on and Knox stepped back from the table, pulled his cell from his pocket, and smiled the kind of smile that made her all kinds of warm inside.

Her phone chimed with an incoming text:

Knox: *Signing shit. Call in 30?*

She tapped out a message back, pulling her lip between her teeth.

Irina: *That's not going to work for me.*

He frowned, pushed buttons on his phone, and her screen lit up. But she was already at the table, so she shouted to him in a French accent, "Sir, I believe it's my turn?"

That's when he looked up from his phone, met her gaze, grinned like he'd won the lottery, and practically pole-vaulted over the table to her.

There was crashing and some shouting. Tanner yelled something along the lines of, "What the fuck?"

She missed quite a bit of the ruckus given that his mouth was on hers, and she was welcoming the kiss. Yes, she sort of missed the rest of the chaos, but there were definitely some catcalls, security got involved, and Knox held her tight, holding her face close to his.

"You're here," he said, holding her face with his hands.

"That's a helluva hello," she said against his mouth.

Cameras were clicking away in the background, but neither of them cared.

"This is way better than anything I could've imagined," Courtney said from somewhere in the distance.

"I did not expect the table jump," Becca added. "I don't think Linx would've jumped over a table for me."

"I totally would've," Linx said from somewhere nearby. "You want me to do it now?"

"Did Courtney know about this?" Knox asked, peppering Irina's face with more kisses.

"Who do you think bought me the sweatshirt?" Irina looped her arms around his neck, and let him nuzzle her.

They got the table righted, he finished signing things, but insisted she stay right beside him while he finished. When the line was done, Courtney handed him a note and a set of keys.

"You've got reservations in thirty at this restaurant. I've already tipped off the paparazzi so they will be meeting you there. Smile lots." She pointed to Knox. "Kiss her."

He did just that.

"I meant in front of the photographers?" Courtney said the words as though she was rolling her eyes.

"Right," Knox said.

"Right," Irina said.

"Don't lose the photographers, okay?" Courtney asked. "But give them a little chase so it looks real."

They could do that. They could totally do that.

Chapter Twenty-Four
KNOX

3 Weeks Later

WHEN THE BAND hit a new city on the tour the whole thing was like a rinse and repeat of the previous town. New faces, same songs. Nothing changed, and everything changed. Through it all, he always wished he was somewhere else with someone else. Wherever Irina was, that's where he wanted to be.

"You okay, bruh?" Tanner asked, heading for the stage.

He wasn't. Something was wrong.

Irina didn't call, didn't answer, and wasn't responding to texts.

"I'm fine," he said, but even he could tell he didn't mean it.

He bounced on his toes, willing his wife to take a back seat in his brain long enough that he could do his performance and then continue with his panic fest.

"Knox, did Irina ever get in touch?" Courtney asked, stepping beside him, bouncing Harley on her hip. Harley was in her concert gear, which was baby ear protection and a super cute onesie that said, *Who's my daddy?* with Bax's face on the front.

Fuck. "She's still not answering for you either?"

Courtney shook her head. "No."

"Are we worried yet?" Knox asked, his hands going to his hips.

"Yes," Courtney added, nodding.

That one word sat heavy in his stomach.

"On in five," Hans said, clapping Knox on the back as he strode by.

"Hey." Knox hurried to keep up with him, pushing through the mass of stagehands and backstage personnel. "Irina's not answering."

Hans didn't even glance over his shoulder as he said, "She's probably on set. They work late. You know this."

"No." Knox moved in front of Hans and stopped, something he never did. "I need you to check in on her, something's not right."

"What's not right is that you aren't at your keyboard." Hans widened his stance, and while his give-no-fucks attitude usually didn't bug Knox, tonight Knox was off kilter.

"Man, you either help me find her or I'm gonna go find her," Knox said.

"You have fifty thousand fans out there waiting. You're not going anywhere." Hans rolled his eyes. "Fine. I'll find her."

That's all he asked. He turned to tell Courtney he'd put Hans on the case when his phone buzzed. He pulled it from his pocket and breathed a huge sigh because the picture he'd taken of Irina over honeymoon bagels filled the screen.

He flicked on the receiver. "Noodle Cup, new compromise, we don't go all day incommunicado. I'm flipping out over here."

"Knox?" a woman who was not Irina said.

"Terri?" She'd picked up Irina's phone enough times, he knew her by name.

"Knox." Terri stopped. "There's been... Irina got hurt."

Everything in his body paused. His blood quit pumping, his neurons stopped firing, his feet wouldn't move. Terri was mentioning something about an accident and falling and a hospital, but the rushing in his skull wasn't allowing him to fully grasp all the words.

Alone in a sea of people, he couldn't make himself move.

"Irina?" he asked her name.

"Knox, did you hear what I said?" Terri asked. "I'll text you the address. They need her next of kin to get in touch right away. You should get here, too, she needs you."

Next of kin... That was him. He was her husband. He had responsibilities they'd agreed to when they signed the marriage license.

Still he couldn't move. "Irina?"

Hans barked at him to get his ass on stage, but even if he was considering going, which he wasn't, his feet wouldn't budge.

Hans started using cuss words, but Courtney cut him off. She slid the phone from Knox's ear, and he still didn't move. His hand dropped and everything turned to slow motion.

"Irina?" Courtney passed the baby to someone as she said, "No, this is Courtney... Who is this?... Oh God."

"Irina?" he said her name again, but there was so much movement going on and none of it was him.

"Hey." Bax was there, smacking Knox's cheeks. "Wake the fuck up, bud."

Linx showed up, too. "Somebody get him some water or something."

Tanner and Mach maneuvered him to a chair, which was silly because he didn't need to sit. He needed to *go*.

"Take a drink," Linx lifted the bottle to his mouth. But he didn't need water.

What he needed was to get his body to move so he could find an airline and get his butt to California to be with his wife. His wife, who was hurt.

"Man." Bax shook him. "She's going to be fine. Irina is going to be fine. Courtney's got the information. She's at the hospital, and she's hurt. They need to talk to you."

"They should call her parents," he said, his feet coming unstuck. He stood. "She'll want her parents. They'll know what to do."

"Hey." Bax got right up in his face. "She needs *you*. Concert's off. We'll re-ticket. Hans is getting us home."

He nodded. "Yeah, she needs us."

"No." Bax shook his head, placing his hands on Knox's shoulders. "She needs *you*. She's gonna be asking for *you*. Can you get your head together enough so we can make this happen?"

He nodded. "Uh-huh."

He didn't. The things that happened after all happened to him, not because of him. He hated that. Despised himself for being a limp lump while everyone worked around him.

There'd been a fall. Her harness came loose on a climbing wall. She'd hit her head, wasn't waking up. Something about Chris Hemsworth, but Knox wasn't sure what that had to do with anything.

He didn't sleep, even though the chartered flight was taking all night. Couldn't sleep, because he worried when he woke up she wouldn't be there anymore. So he stayed up. Drank a fuck-ton of coffee.

"Hey," Bax said, sitting across from him. Linx, Tanner, and Mach all joined him. "What do you need from us?"

"Irina." That's what he needed.

"Yeah, we…got that," Tanner said as Mach shoved him with his elbow.

"I'm not supposed to love her," Knox said, finally looking up from the window into the faces of his friends.

"Look, if we got to pick who we fell in love with, do you really think I'd have picked Linx's sister?" Bax asked. "No, but it wasn't a choice. It happens. It happened to you, and now you know. The good news is she doesn't hate you the way Courtney hated me. I…uh…think you're ahead of the game."

"Did she wake up yet?" he asked.

"No, man," Linx said. "Courtney keeps calling. It's all over social media. Her parents are at the hospital. Apparently, your parents are there too. They all know you're coming. They're worried about you."

"They should worry about her, not me."

"Man." Mach gripped Knox's shoulder. "I know this feeling. That the world just vomited in your face, and you've somehow got to figure out what to do next." He gripped harder. "You just keep fucking going. That's what you do. You do it for Irina. You do it for us. You do it for you. But you just keep fucking going."

"I can't keep going without her." Knox hated himself for it, but he needed her. Even a phone call a day was enough to get him through. If that's all they could have, that's all they could have. He'd live with it.

But he couldn't live without her.

Chapter Twenty-Five
IRINA

FUNNY THING, falling off a mountain hurt like a sonofabitch. The clip came loose, and she tried to fix it, but she should've just let the other guy do it, because then everything was upside down.

Even if the mountain was only a set, and the fall was "only" sixteen feet or so, and they'd had an inflatable bag set up in the unlikely event of a fall...they hadn't expected her to go headfirst.

Leave it to her to take things over the top.

She blinked, then stopped doing that because it hurt worse.

This must be a dream because Knox was right there in her space. Hold up, were his eyes wet? Dream Knox wasn't sobbing, but there was a definite sheen at his eyelashes. That wasn't right. She closed her eyes to lessen the headache.

"Irina." Real or not, Knox's voice was a balm against the headache from hell. "Wake up. We need you to wake up."

"Hurts," she said, keeping her eyes closed.

Dream Knox's hand found hers. That was nice.

Someone else said something, but she didn't really care because it wasn't Knox.

"I know it hurts," he said, seeming to understand she was blocking out everyone but him. "But can you open your eyes for me?" he asked, rubbing at the soft spot between her thumb and index finger.

"No." She wanted to turn her head, but had a feeling that would hurt even more than the blinking thing. "You aren't supposed to be here because you're in Europe. Probably onstage still."

"Irina?" his unmistakable voice slipped through the brain fog. "I'm right here with you. You had a fall. I need you to wake up now."

"You're not real." She shifted on the bed, but that seriously hurt. "Knox is on a different continent."

"I'm here where I need to be," he said. "With you."

"Okay," she said, still keeping her eyes closed. "You can stay."

There was some murmuring and talking. She didn't like the metallic taste in her mouth at all.

"I'm going to sing for you," Dream Knox said. "That okay?"

"Uh-huh." Actually, that sounded really nice.

So he did. The metallic taste got stronger as she slipped into black bliss while he sang her song about a girl with eye color that changed as often as her hair color. She smiled, because even though she was embarrassed as all hell, her head pulsed like she'd fallen off a mountain, and opening her eyes hurt—Dream Knox was there with her.

The days after she woke up the first time stopped sucking so badly because it turned out Knox was the real deal. And he did his best to keep her comfortable. Anytime anyone got near her, he growled just enough to ensure they didn't get on her nerves.

Her parents came all the time. She sort of recalled something about Knox's parents showing up, too.

Then there was some issue she'd heard about too many

guests, but whatever Knox had said or done nipped that in the bud because Courtney, Becca, Terri, Irina's parents, and Knox were all there on the regular.

The guys went back to the tour and Knox had a sub for a replacement until she was better. She didn't like that. Didn't like that he wasn't where he was supposed to be, all because she'd screwed up her clip and taken a tumble.

She was definitely out of service for at least a few weeks more. Brain rest after a concussion of this magnitude was apparently not optional.

Today, though, it was just her and Knox. No television, no cell phone, no books, just her alone with her brain and her husband. Which left her a lot of time to think. Think about Knox and how she'd developed serious attachment. Her attachment to him that brought him all the way across the world when his dreams and his job were on the other side.

She wasn't so worried about herself. Hell, she could take on a whole mountain and still survive. But Knox...she couldn't let him get so close that he'd be trapped.

She didn't want to trap him like his parents had for so long. They'd taught him to forgo his own happiness to earn their love. She wouldn't do that to him. She needed to release her grip and her need, so he could have it all.

It took a little effort for her to focus on him.

When she did?

Holy shit, Knox looked so tired.

He stared at her like she was a ghost. Yes, she understood, this wasn't her best look with the whole brain scramble, a black eye, and poly-cotton hospital gown.

"I look like hell, don't I?" She grimaced.

"You always look gorgeous." He stood, stretched, and moved to her. "Can I get you something?"

"I'm okay," she said.

She was so addicted to the man.

"Does it hurt worse today?" he asked, touching her like she was a thin sheet of glass.

She shook her head. Now, that? That was painful.

"It doesn't hurt when I don't move." She held onto him as much as he held onto her.

"I need to tell you something," he said, right up in her space. "I've been thinking about it while you were sleeping."

"That you got me some more pain meds?" she sort of joked.

He grinned. Leaned in and kissed her temple.

"That I love you," he said into her hair, totally whacking her upside the head with the words.

She blinked. Hard blinks. When he finally released her, she was still in shock.

"You love me?" She frowned. He couldn't love her. Not when she needed him like she did, it wasn't fair to him.

"I couldn't help it." He gripped her hand right below the IV. "You're just so damn lovable."

"Knox, we can't love each other." That would mess everything up.

"I do, though."

"This wasn't ever supposed to be that. We both agreed." She'd worried they were in too deep before, but now she knew for certain they were.

"And that's what you want now?" he asked. "That's *really* what you want?"

It wasn't about what she wanted, it's about what she could have. "Our reality hasn't changed." Had it? Sure, she'd missed him like she'd never expected, but had things changed so much? To be together, someone had to give something up, and no one should give anything up. That was the whole deal from the start. Everyone gained. No one gave anything up.

"What if the things I want have changed?" he asked, stroking her palm. "What if things changed for me when I got a call that you weren't waking up?" His voice broke a little. "I am terrified of what forever looks like with you," he said, the honesty in his words pure. "But I'm more terrified of what forever looks like without you."

"Knox." She gripped his hand. "C'mon…"

He traced the line of her IV, up the vein to her elbow. "I need you, Irina. Not just a call here and there, but…more."

"How can we even make that happen? We're both living different lives."

"What?" he asked. "You want to keep to the original plan? Go back to that?"

"Don't you think that's best?" she asked, wishing she could flip on the light and not get a raging headache from the bright.

He traced the vein back down. "No."

She moved her other hand to hold his still. "What if the longer we hang on, the harder it's going to be when the day it ends comes?"

"What if the day doesn't come?" he asked.

With their schedules? The way their lives were going? There was no way they could keep it up. The day would come. "You said yourself it's only a matter of time."

He didn't release her hand, but it still seemed as though he were slipping away. "So you want to be done?"

No. That's not what she wanted at all.

He reached to her neck with his thumb, seeming to trace her profile. Etching it in his memory or something like that.

She nudged him, just a little. "It doesn't have to be dramatic and it doesn't have to be today. We both knew this was coming."

He stood. Paced to the oxygen tank on the wall, studied it. Then paced back. "And then things changed. You opened up to me and I sure as fuck opened up to you."

That was a mutual mistake. "We didn't follow our own rules."

Now they had to pay the price.

"Right." He stopped. "Tell me you want me to leave, and I'll go. Tell me you want a divorce and I'll sign the papers."

"What I want has nothing to do with this." It didn't. If she got everything she wanted she'd already have five Academy Awards and an Emmy for best actress in a sitcom.

"It has everything to do with it," he said. "You still get your career. I'll make the changes so we can be together."

"You'd give up the band?" she asked, totally appalled that this was even a conversation.

"If that's what it takes." He nodded.

No, that wasn't going to happen. She wouldn't let him do that.

"Your parents twisted you in knots, and you had to allow it because you loved them. I *refuse* to be another person in your life who forces you to rearrange your own happiness because you love me. You love your job, your band…that's who *Knox* is."

He shook his head. Something in him changed as she spoke. Hardened. "Then you really don't know me at all."

"Knox…"

"Do you love me?" he asked. "I fell in love with you, but did you do the same?"

She opened her mouth, but words wouldn't come. If she told him she'd fallen in love with him, too, it would only make everything harder.

"I'm gonna take a breather," he said.

"We can always stay friends, Knox," she said. "No matter what happens. We have that."

He waited a long moment at the door, his back to her, but he didn't turn around. Not even when the door closed. No, he didn't look back.

And she didn't have any idea what she was supposed to do with any of it.

Chapter Twenty-Six
IRINA

"YOU NEVER WANT to talk about it," Courtney said, keeping an eye on Harley as she motored around the floor of Irina's Los Angeles apartment.

Knox left to finish up the tour, but Courtney stayed in Los Angeles to keep an eye on Irina. She, Harley, and Becca temporarily moved into her old apartment, so they'd be close in case Irina needed help.

Becca listened in on their conversation, but kept to herself as she read through some patient case studies for her next seminar.

"I want you to stop being pissed at him." Irina stood at the counter, folding laundry.

She still got headaches, but they were manageable. Mostly, she wished she could cry. Since the fall, she'd needed to, but she hadn't been able to.

"You really want him to file divorce papers?" Courtney scowled. She'd been doing that a lot.

After Knox left the hospital, Irina called Hans and got him back on the tour. Then she pulled herself together, finished her mandated brain rest, and finally got to go home. Now, the bruises were mostly gone, and they'd resume filming in a few weeks. Everyone had to take a break while they investigated the fall.

"He loves you," Courtney said. "He told Bax, and *Linx*, that he loves you." She put an emphasis on Linx to clearly try to loop Becca into the conversation. "So why does a guy who loves you want to file for a divorce?"

"Drop it," Irina said, softly.

"Why?" Courtney pushed.

"Because I love him." That was the end of that.

"You love him?" Courtney confirmed.

Apparently that wasn't the end of that.

"Yes." Irina folded with a little more zest than necessary.

Courtney pretended to do a dot to dot with her finger using the grout on the counter. "He loves you."

"That's what he said." She was seriously starting to think about pretending to have another headache so they could drop this conversation.

"So that's why he's talking about a divorce?" Courtney finished her fingertip dot to dot.

"Uh-huh." That was the simplistic version of what went down.

"That makes no sense at all." Courtney flung her hands wide.

"I don't know, it makes sense to me," Becca said, from the couch. "You don't want to lose him, but you also want your career. You don't want to lose your career, but you also want him. So you decided you can't have any of it by convincing yourself you're doing him a favor?"

"No." Irina crossed her arms. "No."

Holy crap.

"I also don't want him to make sacrifices because he loves me. That's not what love is."

She was nearly certain.

"Shit," she said. "Is that what love is?"

No one said anything, which was plenty of an answer for them all.

"Is this a good time to discuss your reluctance to relationship yourself with anyone romantically?" Courtney asked, careful like this was a minefield.

"It's never a good time for that," Irina said, her throat clogging.

"I kinda want to hear about it," Becca said, gentle and with a slight smile.

"I fell in love once before." Irina swallowed. "He was an actor, too. We were both trying to make it until he decided to give up. Wanted me to come back to Ohio with him to have a"—she made air quotes with her fingers—"real life together."

"He wanted you to make a sacrifice you weren't able to make," Becca said, tilting her head to the side a little. "That's interesting."

"I would've made sacrifices for him, but not that one." Irina shook her head. *Not that one.*

Courtney opened her mouth, then shut it. Then opened it again. Finally, she said, "Someone who really loves you, would never ask you for something that would make you miserable. They'd try to find a way to compromise."

"Like fly all day to see *you* only to turn around and fly back to perform," Becca said, offhandedly.

"Like take the break from filming and make the effort to go where he is," Courney added.

Irina deflated because she and Knox were already compromising, and it didn't suck. It had worked. It'd been hard, but it had worked.

"I think I complicated things," she whispered.

Becca highlighted a passage on the pages in front of her. "Because you want to have a career *and* have him? Did you ever tell Knox you want both?"

"Of course not, I can't tell the guy he has to make sacrifices so we can be together, and I can also have my career." That wasn't nice, and it's what her ex had done to her. She gulped.

Becca looked up then. Set the papers aside. "Are you still willing to make sacrifices for *his* career?"

"Like going on tour and stuff?" Irina asked.

Becca nodded. "Like if he's got a big career thing, are you willing to make it so he can have his moment if he's willing to do the same for you when it's your turn?"

"Of course, I just can't ask him to give me my turn."

"Why the hell not?" Courtney's frustration was clear in her tone and the way she smacked herself on the forehead.

"Because it wasn't what we agreed on!" And now the headache would probably truly start in earnest.

Becca stood and headed to the kitchen. "But what you agreed on is making both of you miserable."

"He's miserable?" Irina didn't want him to be miserable. She figured he'd have moved on by now. It'd been a few weeks and she'd spent every second of those weeks convincing herself that he didn't really loved her. That the feelings were the passing through kind. Not the stay forever kind.

"When I'm in Denver, I miss Los Angeles," she said. "When I'm in Los Angeles, I miss Denver. I can't win."

"When do you miss Knox?" Becca asked, but she wasn't being a therapist. She was being a friend.

"Whenever he's not in the room with me," Irina confessed. "Messaging me. Calling me. Sending me random MyTube videos he found and thought I'd enjoy."

"I think you broke his heart." Courtney sighed. "It doesn't matter where you are in the world—Denver or Los Angeles— you'll always be the one who got away." She paused. Licked at her lips. "That'll be who he is for you, too."

"Unless," Becca put her forearms on the counter. "You go back and tell him you are ready to have a marriage where you both decide things as you go, and not with predetermined contracts at the beginning."

"You are clearly not a fan of predetermined contracts…"

"You got that, eh?" Becca shook her head a little. "They never work out."

"I never actually *made* him pie." Irina dropped to one of the counter stools. "I bought him pie. I always promised to bake, and he did write me a song. Yet, I didn't do it." Oh great, now the tears would come. "I owe him so much pie."

"For clarity's sake, are we being literal here or is this a metaphor?" Becca asked in that way of hers that was both pure calm and also frustrated query.

"Literal." Irina could not believe she'd messed things up so badly. She couldn't even blame the fall. Could she? "Can I blame the knock on the head for this lack of judgement?"

Courtney and Becca both gave her matching you've-got-to-be-kidding glares. Of course she could. This was Knox and she loved him.

"Okay, so I need to start baking and figure out how to get to Amsterdam." So she could make things right with the guy who actually might want to be with her forever.

Chapter Twenty-Seven
KNOX

"YOU KEEP up that attitude and they're going to take away my asshole card to return it to you," Mach said, standing beside Knox, making rock 'n roll devil horns while the photographer clicked away.

Knox grunted in reply, but didn't say anything.

He hadn't said much since he'd left Irina's bedside and gone back to work.

Now everything tasted like he'd eaten a pack of cigarettes, and he wasn't sleeping. Since he wasn't sleeping, he had lots of time to think about her.

They took about a million more pictures with the VIP crowd, before Hans finally called it and sprung them so they could go back to the hotel.

Usually, staying at a hotel was a highlight of the tour. A break from the buses, room service, a shower big enough to actually stand up in.

Tonight, the hotel was just another bed in another city. Another night that didn't matter.

"You wanna grab a bite together?" Bax asked.

"Or a beer?" Linx added.

They were only being nice to him because they felt bad.

Their wives were both meeting them at the hotel. He hadn't asked how Irina was doing, how she got along after the fall, and they hadn't offered.

"Nah. I'm gonna crash," he said. Maybe he'd clean out the mini bar and binge on whiskey and pretzels before he hit the bed. More likely he'd just lie there and stare at the ceiling, wondering what Irina was doing. Where she was. If she was okay.

The crew had already dropped his suitcase in his room on the top floor across the hall from the other guys. So he used his keycard, figuring maybe he'd hit the bar downstairs and talk to someone who didn't feel bad for him. But immediately tossing that option, because he didn't really want to talk to anyone.

The lights already burned in his suite, and there were candles lit.

"What the fuck?" he said. Everyone knew a guy in the middle of a breakup didn't want candles in his hotel room.

"Hi." A voice he recognized immediately, but didn't expect to hear sliced through the space between them.

He didn't want to turn around, because she was there, and she was probably there to be his friend. But the masochist he was to himself had him turning her direction, wanting to hop over all of the furniture between them to wrap her up in his arms.

"Hi," he said, instead of the other things he wanted to say. The things about missing her, loving her, and worrying about her. Or even a simple hello.

"I don't want to be your friend." She'd kept his Whitesnake shirt and had it on.

He hated how good she looked in it. The woman could pull off jeans and a Whitesnake tee like nobody's business.

"Okay." He headed to the mini bar, making the decision on the fly to get slithered and pass out.

"Knox," she said his name in a way that made him go still. "I love you, too."

His throat clogged, and the light from the candles bounced off the walls. The woman he loved stood across the room, and she loved him, too.

"I've been baking for two days straight," she went on, the large room feeling smaller. Comforting. "And getting this number of pies through customs was not a small thing."

"What are you talking about?" he asked, really looking at her this time. Letting himself savor all the parts of her.

"I screwed up. I got scared. I didn't want to be another person you love who takes advantage of it."

"You didn't want to take advantage of me?" That was the stupidest thing he'd heard all year, and he'd spent a solid amount of time with Mach and Tanner, so he'd heard a ton of stupid shit.

"It doesn't make sense, I know." She held up her hands. "But it's the truth. And I didn't want to admit that I love you. That I need you. Because I think I need you more than you need me, and that scares me."

"I haven't slept." He didn't dare take a step toward her, but the room still seemed to shrink between them. "The guys make me eat and nothing tastes good. I think about you and my brain goes numb. But you think I don't need you?"

"I think I got confused." She licked at her lips, wetting them. "Because now I know we need each other."

"Where does that leave us?" he asked, afraid of the answer, but needing it all the same.

"I'm hoping," her breath seemed to catch, and her words cracked. "I'm hoping we could actually stay married. I have an entire closet at your house waiting for me. I just… I don't want to hurt you."

Hands on his hips, he stared at the beige hotel carpet as something cracked inside him. Something that he hadn't realized had hardened.

"Our house," he said. "Community property, and all that. It's *our* house."

"I love you," she murmured.

"That's the best news I've heard in a long time, Noodle Cup." He didn't grin, but he didn't frown either. This was happy. This was perfection.

"I made you so much pie," she said. "So. Much. Pie."

"I've been promised a lot of homemade pie for a while now," he said, sauntering toward her. "But it never comes through."

"Oh." She looked up at him as he got closer. "I came through."

He touched the side of her temple. "Are you okay?" he asked, gently. "I close my eyes and see you falling. I can't breathe when I think about you hurt like that."

"I'm fine. My skull is remarkably dense, it turns out." She smiled and lifted up on her toes to brush her mouth against him. "That came in handy."

He'd been pretty certain that the butterflies-in-his-stomach days were over, but there they were. She kissed him and he got all kinds of butterflies.

"What comes next?" he asked. "After the pie?"

"We could make plans, but sometimes you plan a big white wedding and still wind up in a red dress getting married on a pirate ship." She stepped closer to him. "And that turns out pretty epic."

"We do have a lot of fun," he said.

"You asked what happens next? I have to finish filming while you finish the tour. Then after we meet back in Denver and when opportunities come up, we coordinate so we're not away from each other for so long."

"I like that plan." He wrapped his arms around her, holding her against him, letting the pieces of his life click into place and all the extra bullshit fall away.

"I'm not giving up my career, but I'm not giving you up either," she murmured.

"That's good, since I'm not giving up my career, and I'm not giving up on you either." He pressed his lips to the crown of her head. "I also did something today that I thought you'd like."

"Yeah?" She snuggled against him in that way of hers.

"Mom called and asked me to fly to New York to meet with some bigwig she needs on her side. He's a Dimefront fan. I told her she could bring him to a concert, but that's it."

"You seriously did?"

"I even answered her call on the first ring and didn't panic about the birds chirping." He waggled his eyebrows.

"Now that *is* progress." Somehow they were going to make this work, he had faith in that now.

"I love you, Knox," she said against his shoulder.

"I love you, Irina," he said right back.

They stood that way for a long, long time. Grasping onto each other and not letting go.

But when they finally did, she showed him to the bedroom, where she'd laid out more pie than he'd ever seen in his life. There was cherry, apple, blueberry, chocolate, vanilla, butterscotch, even a pizza.

"That is a lot of pie," he said.

"Promised and delivered." She squeezed his hand.

Yeah, he loved his girl, and he'd keep writing her songs as long as she'd listen because as long as she kept making him pie, he'd keep eating it.

Which was, for clarity's sake, forever.

Epilogue
IRINA

SOMETIMES WHEN FORMER Dimefront band manager, Brek, had staffing issues, he'd have the guys help him out behind the bar at Brek's Bar. The guys loved it, and the customers loved it even more.

Since Knox and Irina had finished the award show circuit and were looking for something a little lower-key, they agreed to close out the bar tonight. Everyone else had cleared out. It was a Tuesday, so not totally unexpected.

"What are you thinking about?" Knox asked, drying another glass before putting it away on the shelf.

The man could play keyboard, guitar, sing like Bryan Adams, deliver babies on airplanes, wear a tuxedo like nobody's business, *and* tend bar. She'd begun to think there was nothing he couldn't do.

"I've been thinking about a lot of things," she said. "Maybe we should talk about kids and where they fit in our future?"

It's true, mostly these days, Irina had been thinking about babies. Not because it was the cliche next step in their forever, but because she discovered she actually enjoyed them. Babies, that is. Spending time with Harley showed her that being an aunt was awesome, but being a mom might not suck.

"You've been thinking about kids?" he asked, leaning over the bar to press a kiss against her mouth.

"Mmm-hmmm," she said, letting him linger.

"I've been thinking about kids," he said, pulling back.

"Serious?" she asked.

He nodded, with a little wink of a grin. "If you want them. I want them."

She let out a breath through her nose. "I do want them. Maybe one, at least. Two if labor doesn't totally wreck my ability to laugh without peeing myself."

"That sounds reasonable." He strode around the bar and pulled her to stand.

The jukebox played some old country song, and he danced with her, stroking her hair. "One, maybe two. I get to deliver them."

She laughed. "As long as it's in a hospital where there are medical professionals nearby who didn't learn everything they know online, then I'm good with that."

"Then it's decided."

"You know what else is decided?" she asked, glancing up.

"What?" He turned her, then moved her back into his arms.

"I'm putting in my order for an epidural now before we even get to the fun part of the plan." She wiggled her eyebrows.

"You're not even going to let me explain what a cascade of interventions is, are you?" he asked.

Probably not. "Will you use whatever that is to try to talk me out of doing labor without feeling it?"

He nodded. "Yes."

"Then I don't want to hear about it." She really, really didn't.

"Yet." He dipped her. "You don't want to hear about it, yet."

"Maybe we do the fun stuff first, then we get to the nitty gritty."

"One other thing before we seal the agreement," he said, moving her with him.

"Yeah? What's that."

"If it's a little girl we are *not* naming her Jeremy."

She grinned at that. Another thing they could agree on. Look at them agreeing on all the things. "I like Irina."

"There are never enough Irinas in the world," he agreed.

That bought him a lip-lock. A version that she saved for alone time when she got creative with her tongue and her teeth.

Things heated, and it was clear he was about to drag her back to the kitchen to try out the thing he'd been talking about trying on a countertop. But she stilled because there was an elderly lady patiently waiting for them to stop.

Knox didn't remove his mouth even as he lifted his eyebrows in question.

"I think we have company," Irina murmured against his lips.

Clearly reluctant, he released her.

He clarified once that was his least favorite part of any embrace. He didn't want to let her go, not even a little.

But Irina knew this woman. She was a friend of Tanner's —part of the retirement home crew that added booze to all their food. Babushka! That was the woman's name. She asked everyone to call her Babushka—unless she didn't like you. Then she asked you not to call her anything.

"You are Irina, yes?" Babushka asked in a thick Russian accent, as she moved in their direction.

Irina grinned. "I am. And you're Babushka."

Babushka smiled a toothy-as-hell smile. "I am."

"And I have heard so much about you." Irina bounced on her toes, practically giddy with excitement.

An excitement Knox did not echo. Probably because now he wasn't going to get laid in the kitchen.

"Good. Ve don't need introductions." Babushka waved her hand. "Now, about Tanner."

"What about Tanner?" Knox asked, coming behind Irina and wrapping her in his embrace. She loved that he got to do this now, and they didn't stop when they were alone.

If anything, that's when things got interesting.

Like when he showed her the really good alone-time stuff —things that involved Twizzlers and glow sticks. She agreed not to judge it until she tried it, and then afterward she definitely made him promise to do it again.

"Ve have made his match." Babushka pressed her hands together in front of her chin. "He vill be so happy."

"Does he know you've made his match?" Irina asked, carefully. "Because that seems like something he should be involved in."

"Darling, no." Babushka shook her head. "His match is made, now he must do his part."

"Then what do you need from us?" Irina asked, glancing over her shoulder to Knox.

"Now, you do your part." Babushka rubbed her gnarled wrists together and grinned. "It vill be fun, no?"

"Oh dear God," Irina said under her breath. She'd heard about Babushka's brand of fun. Sometimes it ended with bail money. "But what the hell, I'm in."

"Fun is always relative, but I think in this case I am also in on this match you've made." Knox held his knuckles out for a bump.

Babushka did not disappoint.

Oh hell. This was about to get good.

There's more Knox and Irina!

A special bonus scene Christina created especially for newsletter subscribers!

Claim the bonus scene at:
christinahovland.com/married-bonus

Acknowledgments

Every book holds different challenges for me as an author. In this case, both Knox and Irina have very strong personalities and convincing them to behave was quite the task. In the end, I think they are two of my favorites. (Not that I get to have favorites, but if I did... well... you know.)

Thanks, as always, to my family: Steve and all four of our children. Mom, thanks for giving me a writing cave to escape into. Sereneti, thank you for always enjoying my stories and telling me so.

Thank you to my critique team and beta readers: Tara Wine-Queen, Serena Bell, A.Y. Chao, Dylann Crush, Patricia Dane, C.R. Grissom, Jody Holford, Deb Smolha, Renee Ann Miller, Courtney Lucas, and Becky Wesnidge.

Thanks always to the fantabulous Dr. Victoria for always seeing to the medical needs of my fictional characters.

Emily Sylvan Kim, agent extraordinare, thank you so much for all you do for me and my books.

Holly Ingraham, we've done it again! I adore working with you and am grateful you are my editor.

Audrey Nelson, thank you for the awesome copy edits!

Shasta Schafer you are the bomb diggity when it comes to proofreading. Thank you, thank you!

Thank you to Autumn Gantz my publicist and manager. She's the one who keeps things moving with Team Christina.

Kalie Holford, thank you for your help with managing my social media and for being on Team Christina!

Kirsten, thank you for all you do for me!

Karie and Kiele—thank you for being my most excellent support team.

Denise Allen—my friend and supporter—thank you for loving my books and always being there for me.

Thanks to the team at Audibly Addicted for the fantastic narration and audiobook production. Kim, Mo, Desiree Ketchum and Joe Arden—you are true rock stars.

Thank you to Eric McKinney of 6:12 Photography for the fabulous photo of Jason D. I got to use for this book.

And thank *you*, yes YOU, for making my dream of being an author a reality. This is a pretty great job I've got!

About the Author

Christina Hovland lives her own version of a fairy tale—an artisan chocolatier by day and romance writer by night. Born in Colorado, Christina received a degree in journalism from Colorado State University. Before opening her chocolate company, Christina's career spanned from the television newsroom to managing an award-winning public relations firm. She's a recovering overachiever and perfectionist with a love of cupcakes and dinner she doesn't have to cook herself. A 2017 Golden Heart® finalist, she lives in Colorado with her first-boyfriend-turned-husband, four children, and the sweetest dogs around.

ChristinaHovland.com
Twitter.com/HovlandWrites
Facebook.com/HovlandWrites
Instagram.com/HovlandWrites
Goodreads.com/HovlandWrites
bookbub.com/profile/christina-hovland

April May Fall Sample

**Turn the page for chapter one of
April May Fall!**

About the Book:

April Davis totally has her life in order. Ha! Not really. Yes, she's the Calm Mom—a social influencer with a reputation for showing moms how to stay calm and collected through yoga—but behind the scenes, she's barely holding it all together. Raising tiny humans alone is exhausting, but that's just the chewed-up cherry on the melted sundae of her life. Her kids aren't behaving, her husband left her for his skydiving instructor, and her top knot proves she hasn't show-ered in days.

Then a live video of the "always calm" April goes viral...and she's most definitely *not*. Enter Jack Gibson, April's contact at the media conglomerate that has purchased April's brand. The too-sexy-for-his-own-good Jack will help clean up April's viral mess, and even work with her to expand her influence, but toddler tea parties and a dog with a penchant for peeing on his shoes were definitely not part of the deal.

Now April's calm has jumped ship quicker than her kids running from their vegetables. Not to mention, the sparks flying between her and Jack have her completely out of her depth. Forget finding her calm—April's going to need a boatload of margaritas just to find her way back to herself again.

Chapter 1

APRIL MAY FALL

"Motherhood is not the same experience for every person. It's not even the same experience for yourself when you have more than one kid. Just do the best you can."
—*Jennifer, Maryland, United States*

April

APRIL DAVIS USED to be a catch.

Or at least that's what her husband used to say. But once upon a time was a long, long time and one *very* final divorce ago.

A year ago. Her divorce had been finalized exactly one year to the day.

She gulped down all the emotion from the past year like it was a soda at the 7-Eleven near the yoga studio where she taught classes on Tuesdays and Thursdays. Then, for the briefest of seconds, she honored the memory of what should have been… before refocusing on the future.

She had to honor that now instead.

Cell pressed to her ear in her suburban Denver kitchen, April listened as her social influencer team manager gave her last-minute updates before April left for her livestream that afternoon.

Meanwhile, she eyed her eight-year-old daughter, Harmony, as she forced her feet into one-size-too-small bright green dressy shoes that didn't match her orange outfit. They didn't match at all.

April shook her head frantically toward her daughter, gesturing at the shoes.

Harmony was patently ignoring her mother's attempts to get her attention. Her daughter might as well be coated with an entire pound of butter, because the worries of the world always slid right off her.

These days, between teaching yoga, starting her new business, and wrangling her kids, April barely had time to grab a shower and comb her hair. Or clean her house. Or mow her yard. Her nonstick coating had deserted her right along with her original life plans.

April tried to follow along with the call, but her primary concern at the moment was getting Harmony's cooperation to wear the black patent shoes April had laid out earlier. She had already caved and approved the orange outfit, even though it didn't match the blue the rest of the family wore.

She pulled the phone away from her ear and put it on speaker so she could use both hands to help Harmony.

"These squish your toes," she whispered, keeping one ear on the phone and both eyes on her daughter.

"They make me feel special." Harmony raised her gaze to meet April's with a silent resolve that April felt clearly in the depths of her bones.

Fine, if green pinchy shoes made Harmony feel special, then what did it really matter?

April's teeth seemed to find her bottom lip all on their own, chewing the lipstick clean off. Which meant she'd need to reapply before she left. The mental list of things to remember as she got out the door and stepped into her future as a social media influencer was growing by the second.

"April, you are doing fantastic." Jack Gibson joined the call, his voice throaty and deep. All business. Just before her divorce finalized, Jack was the man who had brokered the deal that would, in theory, make her a household name. He'd arranged a guest spot on the ever-popular, live morning web show *Practical Parenting.* Two weeks to the appearance that would propel her to household status.

Network morning talk shows had nothing on the audience of *Practical Parenting*. Or so Jack said. April had seen the statistics of their audience numbers and they were big. Massive. So she believed him.

"Hi," Harmony said as she skipped to the phone April had placed on the counter. "Who are you?"

Damn. Damn. Dammit.

Was it inappropriate to put her hand over her kid's mouth?

Yeah, April gritted her teeth. Inappropriate.

"Mommy's on a call," she said instead, holding her finger to her lips. "Shhh."

"This is Jack," Jack said, like this was an actual introduction. "Who is this?"

"That's Harmony," April said, pressing her fingertip harder to her lips. "She's getting ready for the big shopping trip."

"Wanna see my loose tooth?" Harmony asked, reaching into the depths of her mouth to wiggle at the molar.

"It's not a video call," April said, shaking her head frantically. "He can't see your tooth."

April hated live videos. Too many variables. Oh, sure, she did them. Of course she did—she had to. But she did them in the relatively controlled environment of her home after rehearsing multiple times. And, also, most of her videos were prerecorded. Life was easier that way.

Even when it was freaking hard.

"I'm wearing my green shoes." Harmony climbed up on the stool to get closer to the cell.

There was a bit of a pause.

"Green shoes are…great," Jack finally said, sounding excessively out of his depth.

If he saw the dress they went with, April had a feeling he'd change that tune real quick. Jack was all about appearances.

He went on about final touches, while April shooed Harmony toward the door.

A success in the world of turning social influencers into celebrities, Jack's blond-haired, blue-eyed, sun-kissed California handsome was wrapped up tight in a suit that probably cost more than her monthly mortgage. At least, that's how his photo appeared on the company website. Still, he had a way about him that soothed frayed edges.

She used to be that way, too, back in the before times. Before the divorce times. She used to soothe, too. Now, though, her edges stayed consistently frayed. Not even Jack could smooth them.

So she did what her mama and her mama before her did: she faked it. Until she made it. Dear God, please let her make it. *The Calm Mom: Mindful Motherhood, Simplified.* Her brainchild and the vision that made *her* feel special. She had become a brand. A brand she'd spun out of nothing but sheer determination and the hope that someday her life would, in fact, be peaceful again. Soon.

Soon-ish. Someday.

Maybe starting today, with this hopefully-leads-to-more-endorsements video of her shopping excursion at Earth Foods, Denver's premier organic grocery store chain.

April's company had launched only two months ago. Over twenty-thousand MyTube subscribers practiced yoga with her prerecorded videos every week. Also, she posted a biweekly meditation series that had surpassed the number of yoga followers within the first month.

Self-sufficiency as an influencer was on the horizon.

Take that, Kent. That'd be her ex. She'd make this work because she didn't need him or any future spousal support.

Back in the day, she'd made the wrong choice to put her career on hold so *he* could play alpha male and climb that corporate ladder. This would be her comeback. She would be her own alpha this time. Alpha, beta, omega…she could be everything.

Harmony bounced out of the kitchen as Jack said, "Your brand is solid. Your content is spot-on. Now *we* shine."

We. As though they were a team. Which, they sort of were, given that he was the Vice President of Influencer Strategy and she was officially now an influencer. With followers and everything.

She took him off speaker and held her phone against her ear as she lifted toddler Lola from the toy-mess she'd made on the floor and began shooing Harmony toward the garage so they could load up.

"Rachel will meet you at the store. She'll ensure everyone is briefed and ready to roll," Jack's words were smooth as honey, calming as a well-timed Savasana. "You have any problems, I'll be right here to help."

"Perfect." April gulped, stepping around a pile of Legos in the laundry room so she could slip into her own shoes, the black flats that would've matched Harmony's.

She switched the phone to her other ear as Jack-the-multi-tasker shuffled papers in the background and said something to someone else in his Los Angeles office she knew he rarely left.

"I can't ask her that," Jack said, but clearly not to April. There was some mumbling in the background before he said,

"Are they willing to pay for it?" More mumbling. Then to her: "They're asking that you bring the dog, April. The store's got a whole canine-food-delivery thing going to the picnic tables out front. They want to highlight it. I'm just finding out."

April's pulse paused a beat. *It's okay, girl. Pick your battles.* But. Uh. No. No. No. April's geriatric basset hound, Mayonnaise—yes, that was her official name—had an unholy fear of riding in the car and a seriously unreliable bladder.

Any outings with Mayonnaise required a solid strategy, not to mention two adults to lift her into and out of the car.

"I…I'm sorry, Jack, but that's not going to happen," April said, glancing at the hefty dog. Mayonnaise chilled near the bay window overlooking the crinkled leaves dropping from the trees onto the trampoline in the backyard.

There was a long pause on the other end of the line. Like he was waiting for her to change her mind.

Jack rarely heard the word "no" from anyone; she was certain of that. Yet, in this case, the no remained a total necessity. Mayonnaise was not invited to the grocery store.

"She just doesn't do well in public," April went on. "Maybe Rachel will let me borrow one of her dogs?"

Rachel was April's assistant and Jack's sister—that's how they'd connected. Rachel had started doing executive assistant work for April, and then she'd introduced her to Jack. Then Jack mentioned her to the CEO of his social influencer management company and things took off from there.

Rachel also had two golden retrievers that were rambunctious, but at least they had solid bladder control.

"Good call," Jack said, offhandedly. "I'll figure something out." There was more shuffling on his end, followed by a muffled, "We need a dog for the shoot. Get Rachel on the line."

"I'll have to add the new dog to the blog, podcasts, social media." Tension infused April's words as she spoke. No way was this going to work.

"April." Jack was back. Jack and his no-nonsense, make-things-happen energy. The energy that had gotten April to sign with his firm. "I solve problems; it's what I do. I've got this. We'll get through the video, then we'll deal with the rest. One thing at a time."

Great. Okay, this was good. *Everything's fine.*

"I'll be watching. Monitoring the comments," he said, his words so smooth, they could melt the glaze clean off a doughnut— the glazed kind with chocolate frosting and little pink sprinkles. Not that April was picky about her doughnut choice.

Except, fine, she was totally picky about her doughnut choice.

Mostly, she had to be, because she rarely ate doughnuts. Until recently. "Recently" being a year ago when her husband — ex-husband—abandoned their family in favor of his midlife crisis skydiving instructor.

She had learned two lessons from her divorce. One, go with your gut before you saunter down the aisle with the wrong man. Even if you're positive you love him and he loves you. That little niggle of doubt? Trust it.

And two, if you don't and do it anyway, then ensure your name is on *everything*. Or he'll be able to take it all with him when he walks away.

"I've got this." She kept the smile in her voice, even as her peripheral vision caught her five-year-old son, Rohan, lapping up Goldfish crackers with his tongue from the garage floor near her van.

He did a leapfrog hop as he flicked his tongue to the nearest cracker.

"This is going to make your career," Jack assured. "Trust me."

"I'm leaving." She averted her gaze from her frog-loving son so she could focus on Jack. "Getting the kids loaded."

As soon as she got the floor-cracker out of her son's mouth. The kids shopping with her was part of the deal with the promotion she'd agreed on. A simple ditty following a peace- filled single mom as she joyfully shops for organic carrots with her well-adjusted children and pretend dog. Today's little side gig Jack had booked for her would be enough to pay her mortgage that month and, hopefully, lead to more.

More being the self-sufficiency she craved.

"I'll call you after," Jack said like the hotshot mogul he totally was. Then he rehashed the specifics and reminders about what she needed to say, not say, do, and not do.

Her muscles tensed at the number of his instructions. She exhaled and focused on progressively relaxing the muscles in her back. This was only a video. One video. Nothing more. She'd done videos before. Everything would be hunky-dory.

"Ribbit," Rohan said, his enormous eyes looking up at her.

April turned back to him, catching him mid-tongue-flick with another cracker from the floor.

Dammit.

Rohan was processing his dad's betrayal by pretending he was a frog. This had concerned her at first, but the professionals assured her he wouldn't be an imaginary amphibian forever. He'd come around; he just needed to know he was loved and life would continue even without his jackass of a dad.

Not that she thought about her ex often anymore. She didn't see him in the faces of their three kids like she used to. The sparse amount of time he spent with them made this task easier.

"April?" Jack asked. "Are you with me?"

Crud, what had he been saying? "Yes, of course. All good."

Hopefully, he couldn't tell she was only yea far from a total freak-out.

"Questions?" he asked.

"Nope," she said, but didn't move. Instead, she took the deepest, most cleansing breath possible and paused, letting her mind briefly sweep clean of all thought. "I'm ready," she said, her voice radiating calm while inside she tried to remember if her older daughter had softball practice the next evening.

It was Jack's turn to pause. There was the sound of paper shuffling followed by, "I'll stick close to my phone while they're filming. Questions, just have Rachel call."

"Of course," April replied, steeping her voice in what, she hoped like hell-o, sounded like "peace-be-with-you" and not "son of a bitch I've gotta figure out how to get my five-year-old to stop licking cracker crumbs off the ground."

"Great," he said. But it came across more like "fantastic." Brilliant. Wonderful.

Breathe in Jack's promises. Breathe out hesitation.

"Great," April echoed, her voice as pure and gentle as a woman who was faking it for all she was worth.

They ended the call, and she gripped her cell in her hand. She held on to more than the phone. She latched on to the idea that there could be more to life than falling, and that made her heart-space soften and her breaths come more evenly.

April brushed a chunk of hair from her forehead where it flopped. This was her life, and she totally had this.

Enjoyed the sample?
April May Fall is Available Now!

—

Played by the Rockstar
Sample

**Turn the page for chapter one of
Played by the Rockstar!**

**He's a rock star.
She's a waitress.
He's about to rock her world.**

Certified behavioral counselor (and former band groupie) Becca Forrester needs a break. Taking a leave of absence from her job, she moves into the apartment over her parents' garage, and clinches a gig waitressing at a dive bar known for bringing in big name musicians.

Cedric "Linx" Lincoln is a certified rock star. Bassist for the hugely popular rock band, Dimefront, he's in Denver while the band is on hiatus a-freaking-gain. He's looking for something—anything—to keep him occupied until they can all get back to making music. When he saunters into his friend's bar, he finds the perfect diversion.

Becca's presence is a breath of fresh air. The sizzle she ignites in him is precisely what he needs. Bonus: no-stress, no-strings hookups are his specialty. But when things between them tip toward serious, his band implodes, and Becca's leave of absence ends, they're forced to decide what their "real" lives should look like. Maybe there's room for an encore…

Chapter 1
PLAYED BY THE ROCKSTAR

Becca

NEON BEER SIGNS totally signaled a new beginning. Sure, a girl might not think it possible, but Rebecca—Becca—Forrester was out to prove they could. The scent of hops and bourbon paired with the blast of music through the speakers and constant hum of life in the background at Brek's Bar in Denver, Colorado. Outside, the snow had turned to a slushy mess. Inside, the bar warmed her like she'd taken a shot of top-shelf whiskey.

Oh yes, this joint was the perfect place for a fresh start that did not involve anyone else or the baggage they dragged along with them.

"Why do you want to wait tables here?" Brek asked, giving a dose of emphasis on *here*. "I'd have thought you'd prefer some place with tablecloths."

Becca laughed. Brek was as biker as biker got—long hair, leather, and an abundance of tattoos. His wife was…not. She was a financial planner, and Becca's friend.

Becca shook her head. She definitely didn't want to wait

tables anywhere else. "I'm looking for the diviest dive I can find."

The idea to wait tables was a complete one-eighty from her recent past as a certified behavioral counselor, but she wouldn't go back. Not yet. Especially not when she was having a perfectly lovely time at the local go-to spot for great music in Denver, hanging with her friends, and harassing Brek into hiring her as a part-time waitress while she took a life break.

"Diviest dive? Well, I guess this is your place." Brek flashed her a smile.

"Exactly." Becca tucked a lock of her thick, brown hair behind her ear, where it belonged but never stayed. "Until I figure out what comes next for me."

"You can live the dream right here with me." Brek patted the bar top like it was a living, breathing thing. Something he adored.

Sigh. Someday she wanted someone to look at her like Brek looked at his wife and his bar top.

Not now. She was on a break from all of that—the relationships, the responsibility, everything—but, someday, the adoration thing would be fun to have, too.

He'd created the perfect dive bar atmosphere—neon lights on the dark wood over the bar with his name lit up in blue. The wood paneling covering the walls was new enough to make the place look well-kept but beat up enough that it didn't look like he had tried too hard. Aesthetically, nothing matched. Yet everything still worked together. The place was definitely Instagram-worthy.

The darkened room hopped in preparation for the band to take the stage. A vibe she loved pulsed through the air. That feeling right before music blasts and the lights come to life. Yep. This was exactly what she wanted for her present life: loud music and the familiar faces of the bar's regulars, with no further obligation for the mental or physical well-being for those around her.

Also, the best bands played at Brek's Bar. Sometimes, because he had the connections, Brek brought in huge names. Like *huuuge*. Waiting tables here was perfect for a recovering groupie on hiatus from life.

"You can start next weekend?" Brek asked.

"Next weekend would be perfection." Becca glanced at her friends, mingling across the room.

Then *Linx* entered Brek's Bar. Becca choked on nothing but air.

Linx. Walked. Through. The. Door.

Bassist for Dimefront. Hot as all hell. Heartbreak in leather pants when he took the stage.

She, on the other hand, was only hot when she wore a sweater. Definitely not heartbreak in any kind of clothing. Unless... Could a woman be heartbreak in yoga pants? She was sure that wasn't possible. She shook the thought from her head as he moved her direction.

Her mouth didn't just go dry; her entire body froze in time.

Tonight, he'd ditched the leather and wore shredded blue jeans instead. Lanky, with ridiculously long dark hair, stubble that was a half day away from being a full beard, and all the charisma of a man who could get tens of thousands of screaming fans on their feet with one chord on his guitar. He scanned the room like he owned the joint.

Brek may have owned the bar, but Linx owned the room.

"Looks like my current assignment is here," Brek said, offhand with a touch of growl.

"Linx is your assignment?" Okay, she tried to resist sliding her gaze back to Linx, but she failed. Every woman in the house got the Linx grin as he continued his slow saunter through the room.

"I'm his babysitter..." Brek said, glowering in Linx's general direction.

Crumpet crap-ola. Her blood seemed a whole lot thicker and her skin a whole lot thinner when he sauntered toward Brek... and her. The blue neon halo was a nice touch. Well done, universe. Well done, indeed.

She sighed because.... Linx.

All eyes were on him. Every woman in the room got a solid eye canoodle as he strutted right up to where she stood across from Brek. His eye canoodle could likely get a girl pregnant. She sucked in a breath and braced for her turn.

Linx moved less than an arms-length away, and her heart stuttered like he'd asked her to remove her panties. Surely, he wouldn't recognize her. It'd been years since they partied in the same circles.

She held her breath because she couldn't take the risk of his scent. Not because she had any special superpowers that involved scented rock stars—that she was aware of—but she knew he smelled amazing. Rock star heaven and concerts and something musky, like oak trees in the rain.

"Do you want me to wait for the drinks, or do you want to send them over when they're done?" Becca asked Brek, ignoring the fact that Linx was right-freaking-there doing some kind of intense handshake thing with him.

"You should definitely wait," Linx said, blasting her out of her knickers with that smile of his.

Yes, she often thought in British slang that she'd picked up one summer on a European Dimefront tour. She really took to their language choices. Refined, but still rather raunchy.

Like her. Rather, who she wanted to be.

She slid her gaze up the length of Linx—long and lithe. Not beefcake, but definitely built. He had more of a runner's build. Muscle and sinew, but not overdone.

He leaned against the bar top, a look of pure happiness on his face. This wasn't a cat's-got-his-cream smile. This was a cat's-about-to-play-with-his-dinner-before-devouring grin.

"Becca, this is Cedric," Brek said, slinging drinks like a pro.

Cedric?

Right. Sure, yes, she knew that was his given name. Cedric Sebastian, wasn't it? Last name was Lincoln, and all the original members of the band took a nickname that had an x at the end. Together, they made a triple-x, which they found hysterical, as pointed out in multiple Rolling Stone articles.

"Becca," Linx—er, *Cedric*—stretched her name across his tongue and played it like an instrument.

He held his hand out to her. *What to do? What to do?*

She could touch him. She should touch him. He was expecting her to touch him.

Do something already, Becca.

She was overthinking this way too much. So she gave him a solid handshake.

The way he squeezed her palm was nearly erotic. For no good reason, either. It was just a handshake. He didn't make any lewd gestures or anything.

Still, the bar seemed to zip to a pinprick and focus on Linx.

"Becca is a friend of Velma's." Brek tossed Linx a look like her dad used to give her when he thought she was going to use very poor decision-making skills.

Becca extracted her hand from Linx's grasp. She noted how he kept the touch for as long as she'd allow.

"I like Velma." Linx grabbed a pretzel from the bowl on the bar and flipped it into his mouth.

"I do, too." Brek continued working. "That's why I'm making it clear to you that *Becca* is a friend of *Velma's*. Which means stop looking at her like that."

"Like what?" Linx held up his hands.

"Like you want to make her Denver," Brek said with a growl.

What the heck did that mean?

Linx popped another pretzel into his mouth. Somehow, he chewed, smirked, and smoldered, all at the same time.

"She's not Denver. Denver is Denver. Becca is Becca."

Brek crossed his arms. "You and I need to discuss what you're allowed to do and not do while you're visiting."

Linx held his palm to his heart and wobbled dramatically. "I am offended."

For the record, he didn't sound offended.

"It's not visiting if I bought a house. That makes it my home," Linx said to Brek.

He bought a house in Denver? Huh.

Perhaps Becca wasn't the only one in the midst of reconsidering life choices.

"You *bought* a house in Denver?" Brek asked. "I thought it was a vacation rental."

"It was," Linx said with a shrug.

"The landlord was being a total dick about Gibson, so I made him an offer." Linx did the pretzel thing again.

"Who's Gibson?" Becca asked.

Not that she had any real reason to be part of the conversation, but Linx hadn't asked her to leave.

"His cat," Brek said, arms still crossed.

"He's more than a cat." Now Linx crossed his arms. "So what if I bought one little house so he has a place to live?"

Brek shook his head. "Whatever, man. You do you."

"That's my plan." Linx slid his gaze to Becca. "Unless Becca wants to sit here and have a drink with me? Then we can see what happens."

Linx gave her a charisma-soaked smile.

Ah. There it was, her eye canoodle. She felt that stare deep down in her soul.

Yeah. Total player.

A player who went through sex partners like they were potato chips. This was according to his bandmate, Bax, and general female knowledge when meeting a player of his magnitude.

Back when she'd followed Dimefront concerts she'd had her eye on Linx. Something about him was like a magnet, pulling her in his direction. She had wanted him. Full. Stop.

But Linx was bad news for her. He rocked a total love 'em and leave 'em vibe. The kind that made a girl like Becca—someone who tended to see only the good in people and, therefore, fall for the wrong men—step away. He had just the right amount of baggage for her to want to unpack. And he was exactly the type of guy to pick up those suitcases and leave town right after she committed to the unpacking.

So she kept far away from his wandering gaze, preferring to observe him in his natural rock star habitat, and not let her heart, or body, get involved.

Brek handed a bottle of Coors to Linx.

"I've actually…" Becca jerked her head toward her group of friends. "Got to get back."

"That's a drag." Linx shrugged and gave Becca an extra-long, excessively thorough glance.

She shouldn't have done it. But she did. Yes, she totally canoodled him back.

"Becca?" Brek's voice cut through whatever the heck was going on between the two of them.

Brek had, of course, known Becca during her groupie days. Back then, he'd managed Dimefront and she'd been a Ten, the pet name they called their groupies. The Grateful Dead had Deadheads, Justin Bieber had his Beliebers, and Dimefront had their Tens. She'd spent a summer being Queen of the Tens.

This was not something she shared regularly. With anyone. No one else in her real life knew. Not even her best friends. That summer had been her first attempt at a life vacation. And it'd worked. Lucky for her, Brek didn't, and she was quoting here, "Broadcast shit that wasn't his to tell."

She let out a long breath and turned to Brek. He glanced pointedly to the order he'd prepared.

"Thanks." She snatched the remaining drinks and—and this was the hard part—she walked away without looking back at Linx and his neon halo.

Enjoyed the sample?
Played by the Rockstar is Available Now!

Made in United States
North Haven, CT
01 April 2023

34847660R00157